COCKY
COWBOY

FALEENA HOPKINS

Cocky Cowboy

Cover Image licensed from Shutterstock.com
Cover Designed by Faleena Hopkins
Published by Hop Hop Publications

ISBN-13: 978-1537483160
ISBN-10: 1537483161

Love is a smoke
made with the fume
of sighs.

William Shakespeare

1

RACHEL

As we stroll past a tented farmers market stand overflowing with vibrant vegetables of every color, Ryan too loudly says, "Bullshit way to charge more money for fucking broccoli."

I glance away from a shiny, violet-colored eggplant I was admiring to the hand-written sign Ryan's pointing at: *Organic Or Bust.*

I roll my eyes.

At my boyfriend, not the veggies.

His expression glints with elitism as he mutters, "*Organic's* a crock. Just a new way to get people's money using scare tactics.

He moves on and I follow, itching to remind him of the scientific studies as well as the logic that back up the claim humans should not be ingesting poison that kills bugs.

Or that kills anything else for that matter. Pretty sure killing-agents shouldn't be lightly sprinkled over food I plan to put in my stomach.

I could then suggest he'd never see himself sucking on a roach motel, right? Just nibbling away while shouting at the latest episode of Shark Tank?

But I'm not in the mood for a debate.

Instead I just smile and mark the secret, invisible scorecard I've begun to keep during this weekend trip to Atlanta.

I will zip my trap and bite my tongue while finding solace here in this lovely, sweet-smelling, sun-splashed outdoor market. It's peaceful. People are here to sell things they love to make and grow. It calms my soul to watch them.

Usually when I come to these, even in New York, I realize I'm breathing more deeply than I have in weeks.

Hell, maybe months.

That's what I'm looking forward to. Breathing deeply. Relaxing. Not wanting to punch my boyfriend in the face.

It started when he called my parents' new house they just bought in a lovely upscale neighborhood in Atlanta a 'suburban jail cell.' He did that as the Lyft driver dropped us off. I took the handle of my suitcase and started rolling away without a word, trying to ignore his comment.

I'm very protective of my mom and dad…and of this city, so the scorecard appeared albeit uninvited.

At first my mother beamed at my handsome, lawyer boyfriend like he was a god. "Mom, this is Ryan."

"Well, helllloooooo!"

"Mrs. Sawyer, I can see where Rachel gets her beauty."

Even though only Dad has the Georgian accent, Mom drawled, "Oh, aren't you sweet." She chose that moment to adopt one.

And there I was proudly basking in the successful introduction and tucking my scorecard away for good. Or so I thought.

When they asked why he'd never driven to upstate New York with me to meet them when they lived there, he said, "If it's not in Manhattan I don't go." As they stared at him, in a home in another state altogether (which made no sense under his argument) he dryly added, "Besides, who has a car?"

"You could rent one," my father offered.

"Meh."

I was used to him acting that way, but seeing their faces, I was mortified. Meh???

The evening maintained its downward trajectory.

This list is as follows:

- He didn't open my car door when my dad held Mom's.

- Answered his phone right at the table while I pretended it didn't bother me.

- Checked his work emails about a hundred times, sometimes swearing under his breath and never once apologizing as conversation was suspended.

- Cut me off when I was talking, but didn't notice as my mom's eyes went dead in response.

- Didn't offer to help pay at dinner, which was very weird and awkward on many levels. I started to pull out my card and at my Mom's face, I slipped it back away.

All things he normally does that I never notice, mind you, save for paying for the bill. *That* he always does when we're alone. I'm guessing his parents buy the meal when he goes out with them. But to my parents he just looked cheap.

To watch my Mom's opinion of him disintegrate was painful, and there was nothing I could do about it. With each infraction she shot me aggravated looks that grew less subtle over time until she was flat out rolling her eyes and strumming on the table while my father just glared at the top of Ryan's head since it was once again buried into his phone.

My spirits sunk.

Once your eyes open it's very difficult to shut them. Believe me, I've been trying.

He's at minus twenty-three points now, and it's only Saturday morning. It's not looking good.

However, it's a new day. I have a lot to be thankful for, and can put last night behind us. Ryan and I have a good thing. Every one of our friends in Manhattan thinks so. Until this trip, so did I.

I will enjoy this beautiful market and let all my anger and disappointment slide away like water off a duck. That's the plan as we make our way deeper into the market.

The appetizing sizzles of Crepe Masters get skimmed over by my disinterested man.

So does the sweet aroma of Indigo Bath & Body.

I point to a blacksmith's stand selling abandoned Georgia Railroad nails found and twisted into the coolest bottle openers with his furnaces and tools, photographs of the process pinned to the tent's walls.

"Those look like keys to a fantasy world," I smile.

"No they don't," Ryan mutters, finally spotting something he wants – Banjo Cold Brew Coffee. His sharp brown eyes light up and with a tug of my hand he guides me to the small cart, our fingers loosely together.

Pulling out his Bottega Veneta wallet he asks me, "Want one?"

"No, thank you." A breeze picks up a stray lock of my sandy-brown hair, and I tuck it behind my ear.

Distracted by the smiling hipster asking if he wants cream, Ryan turns around, declines, takes the cup then mutters, "I doubt this'll be as good as New York coffee," heading off like he didn't just insult the guy to his face.

Minus twenty-four points now. Dammit.

I grab a packet of sugar and follow him, irritated to the point where I have to say something. On a forced laugh I mumble, "Baby, you can be a real jerk sometimes."

Laugh or no, there may have been a detectable pinch of resentment in there.

He side-eyeballs me. "What'd I do?"

"Rye, you insulted that coffee guy. And the people with the veggie stand." Off his surprised look, I hastily add, "I get it. I'm a snob, too, but I don't broadcast it."

He chuckles and takes a careful sip, blowing on it first. "Then you're duplicitous."

"Says the lawyer," I smile with a shake of the sugar packet before handing it to him.

His chuckle shifts to full-blown laughter, partly because he loves that I remembered his sweet tooth.

He leans over and kisses me long and slow before

taking the sugar.

Now that kiss was a surprise.

Maybe all we needed was for me to call him on his crap.

As he empties the raw crystals into his paper cup, Ryan smiles his winning grin I fell in love with. "Rachel, the sooner we get back to Manhattan the better. This place, it's too fucking charming for me. I miss the grime."

I smile in an effort to release my mood. "We leave tomorrow evening. It's only one more night here."

"Can't we just go home today?"

From the look on his face he'd eat the cost and jump on a plane if I said yes.

I'm considering it. I'm having a shit time and want to go home, too. But only because of him.

Being back in the city I grew up in is very nostalgic for me and if I were here alone, I'd be having the best visit. Mom and I would be together at this market buying up everything and anything and laughing a lot. I would have had those crepes, for example. I can still smell them. The strawberries and cream beckoned to me and I let them slip by.

After he comes in for another kiss, slipping his arm around my waist, the coffee held away from my Kate Spade dress, I sigh, "Maybe we *should* go home."

"Yeah?"

"But my parents wouldn't appreciate it."

He tempts me, "Who cares what they think," his voice low and husky.

Why the hell not? I feel like something's coming between he and I...or ending. I don't like seeing him how I do now. Part of me wants to rush to the airport and stick us back in New York where we were almost living happily ever after, especially by city standards. Most of our friends are single.

His iPhone beeps. As Ryan steps to the left to read the incoming email, the subject is put on hold.

I look away from him and in the distance, straight ahead, discover I'm being watched.

An incredibly sexy man is intently staring at me from within a neatly laid-out market stand filled with artisan cheeses.

He looks out of place in this city, like he'd be better suited on a ranch somewhere. He's dressed in a denim button-up shirt over equally faded blue jeans held up with a large, horseshoe belt buckle. It's visible only because a small section of his shirt is accidentally tucked in. The sun dances across his striking and ruggedly tan features, the kind of golden skin that only comes from working daily in the sun.

I cock my head trying to figure out where I know him from.

It's like he's daring me to remember.

He crosses his arms and keeps right on staring at me. As milliseconds pass his lips tighten, framed by several days worth of stubble. Emerald green eyes narrow as I hold his gaze.

My heart stops cold.

It can't be him.

No way.

He looks so different now I almost couldn't place him.

But yes.

It's him.

Oh my God.

Ryan swears at his phone as he types a reply with one thumb, but I don't see that because an invisible rope is slowly pulling me toward the man from my past.

An older white-haired lady is ignored as she asks him a question about his specialized product. She turns to see what's arrested his attention so completely and when she spots me in the same daze he's in, she moves to leave.

Neither of us noticed she was ever there.

After all these years…

Staring in wonder I breathe deeply in and whisper, "Jaxson Cocker."

2

RACHEL

The ghost from my past frowns like he can't believe this is happening either. His lips part, but I never get to hear what he was going to say because Ryan has walked up without my noticing and interrupts, quickly mutating the surreal into very real. "Let me guess. Ex-lover."

I wince, but not because he's right. Because for a few moments there I forgot Ryan even existed.

He's wrong, actually. Jaxson Cocker and I were never lovers.

Not really.

We were…friends.

Blinking for some semblance of sanity, I stutter, "What? No! No. We went to grade school together. That's all. Ryan, this is…" Shocked I'm saying his name, I introduce him in a quieter voice, "Jaxson."

Ryan doesn't move.

Jaxson doesn't extend a hand either. Instead he crosses his arms and drinks in my city-man like he's looking at a turd. Jaxson's voice is so deepened from when I heard it last it jars me as he shoots back, "Let me guess. New York."

My wealthy, elitist boyfriend cuts a scathing glance to the modest table of specialized cheeses and knives made with hand-carved black walnut handles. Label tents display the names and prices, and of course the cheese is all organic.

Ryan smirks, "Let me guess. *Loser.*"

Jaxson's jaw ticks. So fast I don't see it coming, he reaches all the way over the table and punches Ryan in the face. And it's one hell of a punch, so much so that fresh coffee splashes everywhere.

"Still a wild card, huh?!" I bark at Jaxson, turning to my boyfriend. "You okay?"

Furious, Ryan cups his jaw as blood starts to drip down his lip from where his tooth cut it on impact. His hand and arm are dripping sugary brown. "You're spending the night in jail, buddy!"

Jaxson's lips turn back in a sneer. "Worth it."

"Oh yeah?" Ryan snarls, pulling out his phone to follow through with his threat.

"No!" I claw at it, but he successfully holds it out of

17

my reach and dials 911 with his thumb, arm high in the air. "Don't overreact! You insulted him and he didn't like it – that's all!"

"Not your ex, Rachel? Huh? Wanna try again?"

Exasperated I shoot back, "I haven't seen him since we were ten!"

"What?" Ryan's fiery brown eyes flicker at this odd piece of truth.

"I'm serious. We were friends as children! That's all! He used to torment me!"

It doesn't stop him. Puffing his chest and turning away, he informs the dispatcher in a booming voice that he was assaulted.

Jeez.

Assaulted?

Really, Ryan?

As an audience grows I wrap my arms around my head, thinking, *this weekend couldn't get any worse.*

A younger vender in the next booth asks, "You okay, Jaxson?"

"I will be in a minute," he cryptically mutters, walking out from behind the cheese table and glancing to me, holding my confused stare.

Ryan turns just in time to see him coming. His jaw drops in surprise as Jaxson raises his fist high and punches hard, knocking my boyfriend to the ground. The phone skitters across the pavement. The paper cup, too, its contents unleashed all over Ryan's favorite three-hundred-dollar shirt.

Encircled by a growing number of gawkers, I'm totally and completely blown away speechless.

With Ryan knocked out, Jaxson turns to me. "If I'm goin' to jail, might as well enjoy the fuck out of the ride." His old oh-so-familiar smirk materializes, emerald eyes sparkling with amusement just like they always did back then.

Instantly I'm flooded with long-forgotten memories.

* * *

"We shouldn't be here!" I whispered, but he would never listen.

"Come on, Rachel!" Jaxson said, his nine-year-old body ducking under the bent chicken wire fence of an abandoned factory.

"We're supposed to be going to church!"

His bright green eyes danced as he waved me in. "No one's gonna know! Watch out for that spider!"

I screamed and ran under the fence in order to dodge the deadly predator. At a safe distance I searched for it and found nothing as Jaxson's laugh sounded behind me. Whirling around, I threw hands on my tiny hips. "There is no spider!"

"Got you here, didn't I? What are you more afraid of, your parents or a spider?"

He took off running.

Which, as usual, made me chase after. "Jaxson Cocker, get

back here!"

"What're you gonna do, Rachel?" he called over his little boy shoulder. "Punch me? Oooooo, I'm scared!!"

My high-pitched voice shouted, "You'll be sorry!"

Though I always threatened that, we both knew I was all bark and no bite. He was the animal, always fearless and loving to ignore what adults told him to do. He made his own decisions and didn't care if people didn't like it. In fact, if they didn't, he enjoyed watching them freak out.

Jaxson was the only boy in our class who always caused the teachers stress. The one who inspired his younger brother Jerald to work really hard to keep up with and sometimes one-up him in pranks and rebelliousness, making Trinity Elementary a Cocker Brothers war zone.

As I rounded the dirty warehouse's corner, hundreds of sunflowers came into view. They had grown freely thanks to the absence of a lawnmower whirring over this property for many years.

Jaxson jumped out with his hands way up. "BOO!"

I screamed and grabbed my scared heart. "I don't know why I hang out with you, Jaxson. You're not nice!"

His grin spread in the most adorable way as he ran a hand through sun-kissed brown hair, the same color as mine. "Really, Rachel? You don't know?"

"I really don't! You're a stinker!"

He smirked, "You hang out with me because you're in love with me."

My jaw dropped in horror. "As if! You only wish! Ha! Keep dreaming!"

"The lady doth protest too much, me thinks," he laughed. "Come on."

Ever since our fourth-grade class's field trip to see Hamlet performed live on stage, Jaxson had been quoting it. He loved to read almost as much as I did, which was what made us friends in the first place. We always fought to answer the questions first in English class, each raising our hand higher in an effort to win. I often won, but not because I was taller. He was the tallest boy in the school. No, I got picked because our poor teacher didn't want to egg him on.

I knew the feeling.

I followed him to the sunflowers, wondering how in the world he'd talked me into being at this forgotten place. Glancing behind me to make sure no adults were around, I worried like crazy. I knew exactly how much trouble I'd be in when my parents noticed I wasn't with Brittany, Heather and Cora.

They'd realize who I was with, and then I'd be grounded.

And yet...there I was anyway.

I couldn't help it.

When Jaxson asked me to do something, I did it.

With two hands he grabbed a perfect sunflower at its base and tore it out of the ground. It was nearly as tall as I was. His face went soft as he offered it to me, spindly roots shooting out the bottom, the top stunningly bright.

"Rachel, here. This is almost as pretty as you."

I took the extended flower with quiet shockwaves running through my little body because it was the first time Jaxson Cocker had said anything sweet to me. I expected his arrogant smirk to appear and for the mockery to ensue, but they remained absent.

The gap between our bodies somehow disappeared and the toes of our sneakers touched. I don't think either of us knew what was happening. We both had confusion on our nine-year-old faces like a magnet had brought us together against our will. I forgot to breathe. He was breathing fast.

And then he kissed me.

It was sweet and soft.

Just a pressing of his lips onto mine and holding there, without moving one bit.

"What are you kids doing!!?" A large man in grey work-jumpers shouted at us, "Get outta here!"

I gasped.

Jaxson grabbed my free hand. "Come on!"

We took off running, the flower bouncing in my grip.

3

RACHEL

"I think you're lying to me," Ryan snarls, shoving his phone in his pocket after answering another work email.

Sitting on my parent's guest bed, I remind him, "You know I moved to New York when I was ten. You think I was pen pals with a boy from grade school? Come on."

He glares at me, dark brown hair and pale skin, perfect. Ryan Morrison's only flaw is his endless ambition, in my opinion. At least that's what I used to think. Now, I guess I have to add 'oftentimes rude' to the short list.

His eyes narrow. "Are you friends on Facebook?"

That's a valid question considering this day and age with so many people reconnecting over the internet, even after decades of never seeing each other. But I have a hard time believing Jaxson Cocker would even be on Facebook.

23

I won't tell Ryan this but I did think of searching for him when it first came out, only I could just imagine him scoffing at social media. He always went the opposite way of people. And truthfully? I like believing that about him, even if it was a belief born of a childhood friendship. I didn't want to alter that by finding him posting about what he ate for dinner.

"No! I've never even looked for him! It was so long ago we were friends, you're worrying about nothing." Off Ryan's face, I motion to his pocket. "Go check my account if you're so worried. You know the password! It's the same as my email. Read all my messages while you're at it."

He cocks his head like he's trying to believe me, but doesn't. Now I'm just getting irritated.

"You know what, Ryan, the people who are jealous are usually the ones doing bad things."

Walking to loom over me with his 6'1" stature he growls, "What are you saying? I'm not cheating on you, Rachel."

"Well, you're not committing to me either."

Oh shit. I didn't mean to say that.

He blinks and steps back to run one thick hand through his hair. "So that's why you shut down on me last night." He glances to me. "I thought you were just being sensitive, but it's more than that. You thought I was going to propose this weekend."

Hearing it said aloud stings. This is not the romantic way I wanted things to go down. Time machine, anyone?

The last thing a woman wants is to bring up the anticipated proposal before the man does.

Time to change the subject back.

"No. It's just…you're making me defend something silly. Jaxson is just a boy I knew when I was a very little girl. That's all. We have no connection whatsoever."

"I saw your face, Rachel!"

My rarely seen temper flares and I shout, "You saw *surprise*! God, get off my case! It's been over twenty years. You would have had the same expression if you saw someone like that!"

Ryan's dark eyebrows are up. He stares at me a hot second then steps closer to run his hand lovingly down my arm, taking my hand and squeezing it. His voice is gentle for the first time since we got home as he murmurs, "Rachel, I don't know if marriage is for me."

Oh my God. Here I was thinking we were discussing Jaxson like he was really jealous, but it was a diversion. When actually he's been inwardly fighting the idea of marriage and using my childhood friend as a scapegoat. Men can be so tricky.

I'm staring at him wondering, holy cow, is this why

he's been extra rude this weekend? To push my buttons? Or because he's unsure of how he feels about me? Testing the water with the parents, observing me in a new environment? Watching me like a parole officer to see if I behave correctly? Learn if he wants me forever? Oh my God.

When a man loves you he *knows* if he wants to put that ring on. And Ryan is telling me he doesn't.

Like I've been slapped and slapped hard, I tug away from his hand, stepping back into the side of the guest bed. "You said…"

"I know what I said, but it's going to be some years before I'm made partner, and I want to offer you more than just *this* salary, especially if we're going to have children."

He looks so sincere that it takes me a second to realize he's full of shit.

4

JAXSON

Across town at the exact same time.

Justin and Jake walk up to my cell. Even though they're my younger brothers, they don't look very much alike, and I'm a mix between the two.

Justin's tow-head-blonde with pale green eyes that he inherited from our father's side. Jake's got the tan coloring, dark brown hair and brown eyes of our mother's side. But they both have the same swagger and smirks, and there's a self-possession we all carry that would make anyone guess we were related, on sight.

In his normal dark jeans and black t-shirt, Jake chuckles, "Just like old times."

"I'm too old for this shit," I toss back, amused and

happy to see them as I rise up. "Did you tell Dad?"

Justin leans on the bars in his navy blue suit while a young, male police officer unlocks the communal cell.

As the rattling key ring echoes off lonely walls, Justin asks, "You think the Chief didn't already call Dad? Because he did. Then Dad called me when we were on our way over."

The iron door creaks open and I give my long body a stretch as I stroll out to freedom. "What'd Dad say?"

"Said, and I quote, 'Of course he gets into trouble after *Jerald* stayed with him. That boy's a bad influence. On everyone.'"

I share a glance with them before I mutter, "Predictable that he blames Jett for this. And that he won't stop calling him that stupid name."

Jake grumbles, "Calling him Jerald is Dad's little dig. I swear he's never gonna give it up. Petty bullshit."

Justin agrees, "It's beneath him."

We all admire our father to the point of worship. That he hangs onto calling Jett by his birth-certificate name is more than a little irritating.

Even Jett admires Dad, despite their feud.

Michael Cocker is loyal, strong and a man of integrity. Keeps his word. Cares about his family and is there when we need him. Everything a man should be. Our grandmother and grandfather did a good job in raising him, if you ask me.

He's a congressman who cares very much about laws and America's lawmakers. He walks the talk and lives an honest life, which he passed onto us.

Jett and his motorcycle club break rules like they never existed. They do it for good reason, to help those who can't help themselves, but Dad can't see that.

We all wish they'd come together, especially Mom. At times when we least expect it they temporarily bury the hatchet. But it's a rare day and it never lasts.

With a wave Justin calls back to the police officer, "Thanks, Eric. You did me a solid. Call me when you wanna grab a beer."

"No problem, Justin," the cop nods. "I thought it was a bum deal anyhow." He stays back to yell at a drunken inmate, "Hey! There's a toilet for that!"

As I collect my keys, wallet and phone from a pretty cop who hasn't decided which of the three of us she likes better, I ask Jake, "Why aren't you on your honeymoon?"

"Got back this morning," he smirks, his mind clearly on a sex-filled vacation. "Dropped my gorgeous new wife at home and ran straight over."

"She pissed you ditched her?" Justin asks.

"First off, I would never ditch her. And second off, she needs a nap after the workout I gave her," he grins.

"Nice," Justin laughs, the afternoon sun hitting our

faces as we head for his Audi.

I glance into its blinding light, my mind on Rachel's hair illuminated by it when I watched her in the market before she spotted me. How she tucked it behind her ear. Her soft smile as she passed by the stands she wanted to stop at but didn't because she was too busy following that dickhead.

Rachel Sawyer. Holy shit. Can't believe I saw her after all these years.

Blinking back to my tow-headed brother, it occurs to me that his twin is absent for my jailhouse breakout. Not normal. They're always together except at work. "Hey Justin, where's Jason?"

"Picking up your booth. His ridiculous Escalade is good for something after all. Can fit all that stuff."

"Lost a lot of perishables," I mutter, shaking my head.

"Nope. I guess you had a friend there who loaded up your coolers so nothing went bad. The guy packed up your tent, too."

"Really? Huh," I mutter. "I just met him today. What a good guy." I pull out my phone and the business card the kid gave me, sending a quick text telling him I appreciate him looking out.

Then I send one to Jason with the address of where he can drop everything off. He immediately texts back:

You got it. Wouldn't want you to punch me.

Chuckling I tuck the phone in my jeans pocket.

Jake, second youngest of six Cocker brothers, holds the passenger door open and has the balls to say, "Get in back, felon."

Sliding my phone into my pocket, I cock an eyebrow at him. "Yeah, right. Oldest gets shotgun. Forever."

"Bullshit." Jake stares at me and sees I'm not kidding. Grumbling, "You suck," he climbs in the back where he can't stretch his legs out. "I'd prefer the Escalade right about now."

As the Audi hums to life, Justin says over his shoulder, "Then go walk to it. I ain't stoppin' you."

I adjust the seat for *my* long legs making Jake swear at me as I hit his knees, which of course gets me laughing.

Justin chuckles as he backs out of the parking space. His voice is somber as he asks, "Okay, what the fuck happened today?"

My smile evaporates remembering Rachel's city boyfriend and how fucking smug he looked. And he was standing next to her like he deserved her. He deserved what he got.

***

Sneaking into the church mid-mass we tiptoed into the back pew, Rachel still holding fast to my uprooted sunflower. It was a wreck from the run. Her always-pink cheeks had deepened to bright crimson and she was silently panting.

So was I, but not from the run.

It was our first kiss.

I was only nine so girls weren't interesting to me.

Except this one.

Rachel could really keep up even though she acted like she couldn't. We had a lot of adventures like this one, minus the kiss, and during all of them she fought me, which made it more fun.

I loved shocking her, too. It was fun making her do things she would never do with those stupid friends she hung out with, especially Cora who was the girliest girl in our school.

I also liked that Rachel was smart and read as many books as I did. We talked about things I couldn't with Jerald because he preferred television to reading.

As Father Joseph read Psalm 23, I stared at her. Her sky-blue eyes were locked on him.

I started to whisper a quote to her from Hamlet, the letter read by Polonius in Act II. It was one of many I'd memorized after our class saw the play at the Alliance Theater. I grabbed a copy from the library and read it before bed for nights on end.

"Doubt thou the stars are fire." Rachel's eyes locked with mine as I continued, "Doubt that the sun doth move. Doubt truth to be a liar. But never doubt I love."

Her color deepened more.

An old man in the pew ahead hissed, "Shhh!!!"

Rachel and I looked at him, then back at each other.

A smile lit up her flushed face, and I reached for her hand. Our fingers clasped then squeezed harder. She tried to show me she was stronger. We always competed like this. As I used all my strength she bit her lips in an effort not to yelp. I leaned in to whisper, "Will you marry me?"

She nodded, and I stopped squeezing.

* * *

Staring into the memory, my voice goes low. "Some New York douche bag called me a loser."

The car is silent until Jake finally ventures to say, "Jax, people don't usually get to you that easily."

"No," I mutter. "They don't."

I know my brothers want me to explain in more detail but they know me better than to ask or expect it.

Truth is they wouldn't know who Rachel was to me. She's the same age I am, and we haven't seen each other in twenty-two years. With Justin and Jake's age differences, it's useless even bringing up her name. Plus, I'm not the explaining type.

Jett would remember her. He'd be just as impressed by this serendipitous run-in as I am.

But he's busy with his woman and she gave him one hell of a ride, so I'm positive his mind is on only one thing now — making sure she's happy and sexually satisfied so she never runs off.

I have to decide what I want to do.

Let Rachel go, or try to find her?

The thing that has me deliberating long and hard is the inarguable fact that she's not single.

I've got the bruised knuckles to prove it.

She called me a wild card and went to his defense. Hell, if she'd done anything else I would've been surprised, and also not respected her since she was there with him. But I saw in her eyes that she cares for the dickhead.

So…what's my next action? I should just let it go.

But I just want to say hello to her.

See how she's been.

No big deal.

That's what I kept telling myself as I sat in that cell, but there's a nagging suspicion that I'm lying.

Rachel is the only girl I never got bored of spending time with no matter how many hours we were together. I enjoyed her company almost more than Jett's, and that's saying a lot. We used to ditch him sometimes because I liked to just sit and talk to her and he was a lot wilder than that. Talking bored him.

I'm not a big talker either, except…with that girl I was.

But I'm not going to chase anyone, am I?

Jesus, what a fucked up thought.

She's taken. I've never been that kind of guy to go after another man's woman.

Especially since I don't need anyone.

I'm happy the way I am.

I've got my land, my home, my animals.

Give me dawn's morning light over an open pasture of lime green grass with my own cows and horses grazing on it, and I'm a happy man.

Never had to seek out a woman. They always fell at my feet. A man has needs and I've acted on them, and I always treat the ladies with respect. I just don't stay long is all.

But for the last few years I've chosen to shove my more primal needs down, preferring to work on my ranch rather than deal with the hassle of a woman losing her shit.

The last one was a year ago.

Short term. Little payoff. Big pain in the ass.

She wanted to lock it down and come meet my parents before two months was up.

No one ever meets my family, but that's true of all us brothers. Jake's wife was an exception. Jett's new woman, the same. But they're forever and my brothers knew it deep in their guts.

Only Justin's twin Jason has ventured to bring a few girls home because he wears his heart on his sleeve, which we want to smack him for all the trouble it gives him and us. But even he stopped doing that sometime back during college.

We're careful.

We have to be.

The women of Atlanta — especially the moms who have daughters — have their sights set on us.

Old money. Politician dad.

Well-respected, philanthropic mother.

All six brothers, successful in their fields, well built and confident.

Some call us cocky.

I call us comfortable in our skins and aware of our worth.

Hell, if I could convince more people to let go of insecurity and just be who they are, I would, but people like to hold onto their demons and that's none of my business. Hopefully they'll catch on sooner rather than later.

Me?

It's a short life.

I just want to work on my land and live alone.

I'm not a game-player.

Not like Justin to my left here. He loves that shit. Probably why he wants to be senator one day. No bigger game than the U.S. government.

As he turns up the music and screeches left onto

Peachtree Ave, my mind is miles away, playing this morning's events in a loop.

It hit me like a thunderbolt when I saw that spark in her eyes. I think sometimes you recognize souls more than faces.

I was looking at a grown-up Rachel Sawyer, my best friend who moved away when we were only ten.

Then that douche bag kissed her, long and slow.

And everything went red.

5

RACHEL

Across town at the exact same time.

"With your bonuses you make over two-hundred-thousand a year," I whisper, unable to believe I'm fighting for this.

I cross the room to stare out the window at Arden Road's beautiful homes with no fences between them, their green lawns vibrant in the afternoon sun. He's silent behind me.

"I make half that on my travel books, Ryan, and with Huffington Post hiring me on for editorials, that's not going anywhere but up. That's over three hundred thousand a year between us. How much do you think it takes?" I look over my shoulder at my boyfriend, desperately wishing for a way out of this discomfort. "People have children with far less."

"Not in Manhattan," he shoots back with finality.

Confused and feeling terribly insecure, I scan his face. "You're saying *years* from now? You don't want marriage until after you've made partner at the firm? You know this for sure?"

With his back against the proverbial wall, he takes a moment to think about it. We're both hovering in the type of awkwardness where your future hangs in the balance.

Ryan holds my eyes. "Yes. That's what I'm saying."

"Wow," I whisper, turning back to the better view. In a daze I watch a soft grey squirrel strolling across the street with no danger of being hit by a car since few come this way. "Well, I don't want to wait that long."

I hear him come over to envelope me in a warm hug from behind. "Baby, what's the rush?"

There's no rush…

Except I don't want to waste years of my life with someone who doesn't want me.

Who, off this example might continue to postpone creating a future together until I can no longer have children.

Men don't have a clock ticking in their bodies.

I do.

While I'm only thirty-two, how many years can I be in

a holding pattern with a 'maybe someday when I make partner' boyfriend?

"There's no rush," I whisper from miles away. "Except, why wait?"

He abruptly lets go and paces. I turn to watch, feeling we have lost *us* somewhere along the way and I don't know when it happened. How did we get here? I know we've been distant lately, but…

"You're putting me in a box, Rach." Jabbing his finger at me, he almost shouts, "And just so you know, you're being like every other woman on the planet!"

Gaping at him I cry out, "Don't play the 'women are crazy' card with me. It is such a cop-out!"

"It's not a cop out."

"I'm not crazy and you know it." My voice goes gentle. "Do you remember that weekend in Martha's Vineyard when we were lying in bed for two days, room service everywhere and you laid it all out for me what we were going to do with our lives together. The kids. The pretty home in upstate New York. I was right there with you on all of that. And you were so happy as you described it all. I'm not being crazy here. I'm talking about things we both wanted."

"We'd only been dating a couple weeks."

"And now it's been two and a half years."

"We were in the honeymoon period."

"Oh my God."

His lips form a thin, stubborn line. "I don't like being pressured."

Groaning, I throw my arms up, completely losing my mind and removing all the stops. "You think I want to pressure you?!! If I wanted to pressure you I'd ask why we haven't had sex in over a month except for that party the other night at my publishers'! I'd say, hey Ryan, I'm spending more time with the barista at my coffee shop — whose name I don't even know — than I am with you!" Shaking my head in disbelief, I quiet my shaking voice. "We are *talking*! About very serious things that need to be discussed. This is just communication which we need to have in order to be happy!"

"I think we should take a break."

My jaw drops. I step back, and I can feel my heart race as I'm waiting for him to take it back.

By the look on his face, he's not going to do that.

I'm about to argue. So close to the tip of my tongue is desperation, but it occurs to me from somewhere deep in my heart that I am not fucking desperate in any way, shape or form.

While I am not perfect, I have a lot to offer and I *am* lovable, dammit.

I don't need to prove that.

It's just a fact.

Every woman deserves to be loved, and I don't need to plead with Ryan or any man. Ever.

So I grit my teeth and firmly say, "Fine."

Not expecting that, he stares at me. "Fine?"

"Yup. Fine. We're on a break. Take all the time you need. Yay us."

Unsure of what to do with my stance he glares at me like he's expecting me to beg or something. Or maybe he just didn't have a plan ready. Who the heck knows? I can see him searching for what to do now and of course he chooses the most drastic action. He goes for his suitcase and unbelievably announces, "Now's as good a time to start as any!"

My heart caves in. "Now?"

His lips go thin.

In the heat of this fight, my parents slipped my consciousness altogether, until this moment when I picture telling them he's left.

"Are you serious? You're leaving tonight? You can't wait one more day?" Off his silence, I mutter in horror, "What am I going to tell my mom and dad?"

"I don't care."

I blink at him, helpless and embarrassed. How can I stop this train from hitting the mountain?

42

Sometimes people just up the stakes to win when they're feeling defensive, so I decide to give in a little to help him put the sword down and stop slicing me with it. "Wow, you're really angry with me. I'm sorry, Ryan. I didn't want to get you this upset." He slowly zips his suitcase shut like I'm getting through to him, so I try harder. "Come on, baby. Please stop. If you want the break, fine. Just stay the night. We'll leave together and have some time to cool down and they'll never know!"

He stares at the bag for a minute, thinking on it. Shaking his head once, he mutters, "No, Rachel. I'll take Lyft to the airport. You stay here and think about what you want."

"What I want?!"

"Yes." His voice is as cold as a New York winter, which is fucking cold, let me tell you. "You know what I want, for things to be as they have been until we're both ready for more. Decide if that works for you."

I can't even speak. I just stand here like an idiot while he pulls out his phone to book the ride.

On his way out he locks icy eyes on me. "Stop trying to box me in."

My jaw drops. He storms out checking the fucking Lyft app on his phone.

As I watch him go I can't help but wonder if there's someone else.

6

JAXSON

All during dinner I ruminated over what I wanted to do about Rachel. I could have gone back up to my ranch by now but I've hung around Atlanta, which makes me uneasy. I usually know exactly what to do. Never been this on edge before, especially not about a woman.

Mom and Dad were happy to have me over and we talked easily about what they've been up to here, how the basement was flooded and all the chaos that ensued. I told them one of my chickens died last week, which made Mom sigh and lose her smile. Had to change the subject to Jake saying Drew needed a nap after the honeymoon.

Dad laughed under his breath and Mom rolled her eyes. "I don't need to know that stuff!"

The subject of my short-lived jail sentence was only

mentioned once, and by my father with his sternest voice. "I trust this won't happen again soon?"

I nodded, but had to stifle a smile, because who the hell knows, really?

After he went to his office in another wing of the house where I knew he'd quietly write his nightly list of tomorrow's goals and people he needs to contact, I stay downstairs and help Mom clean up.

Just when I think I'm going to drop the whole thing and head out for the hour-long drive I hear myself ask, "You remember the Sawyers?"

Pouring herself a third glass of Pinot Grigio Mom frowns, "The Sawyers?"

I lean against a spotless kitchen counter to coax her memory. "They lived two doors down from us when I was at Trinity. You had them over for dinner sometimes."

Her pretty face flickers with recognition. "You mean John and Ellen? I haven't seen them in years, Jaxson. Ellen and I were only acquaintances. She fought me at every turn at the Atlanta Woman's Club." Placing the cork back inside the bottle, she stares off. "God, I'll never forget. You were too young to be aware of it, but those times we had them over for dinner were stiff affairs. Done only to keep the peace." Rolling her eyes to herself, she mutters, "Not that it helped. That woman had it in for me." Mom's volume rises as she returns to the present and looks at me. "I was relieved when out of the blue their family moved to New York. John got a job or something – I can't remember exactly. We lost touch, thank God. Why?"

"Can you check with the club to see if she's back?"

Intuitive brown eyes carefully inspect me before she turns to put the wine bottle back in the fridge. As she walks to it, she says over her shoulder, "I could. But you have to tell me why."

Staring out at the backyard I grew up playing in, I see little Rachel running screaming around the dolphin fountain, with nine-year-old me and seven-year-old Jett, inside it splashing her like crazy.

Smiling to myself as the image fades and the fountain resumes it's aged appearance of today, I mutter, "I'm curious."

On a knowing laugh, Mom crosses the kitchen back to me. "Would this have anything to do with their daughter? The one you got into trouble all the time?"

I can tell she doesn't remember. "Rachel," I remind her.

"I'll take that as a yes." Mom smiles with a twinkle in her eyes. "Let me guess. That's why you were in jail today."

Can't help but grimace at her knowing I was behind bars. "Uh…"

Mom cocks her head. "Your dad tells me everything."

"I don't doubt it."

They've got the strongest relationship I've ever witnessed in my life. Gives us brothers a very high standard to meet, and we all know it.

Mom asks me, "Are you going to answer the question?" with a look like she knows I won't.

"Can you check?"

She shrugs, "Sure."

"Now?"

She laughs and waves a hand at me as she head for the landline rotary-dial phone, a relic of her mother's, which she refuses to part with since she thinks it's kitschy.

Soon I'm patiently watching her chat up a lady-friend who's also the secretary of the club, about little things until she finally gets to the point.

"I know this is going to sound strange, Constance, but have you heard anything about Ellen and John Sawyer?" Her expression changes as she glances my way. "They moved back to Atlanta? How interesting. Well, I'll have to reach out and say hello." After another pause, Mom's laugh reveals her friend remembers the rivalry she and Mrs. Sawyer had. "Yes, well, maybe she's softened in her old age. Arden Road, you say? What's the house number, do you have it in your records?" She writes it down on a slip of notepaper that always rests on the phone-table. "That's a nice neighborhood. Not as nice as ours though." Another laugh. "Goodbye, Constance, don't work too hard. It is Saturday after all."

Mom tears the top sheet off and walks back for her wine glass. "Look at that. The humidity has already caused condensation and I'd only just set the thing down!" Eyeing me like we're part of a secret plan, she whispers, "If I give you their address, will you be in jail again later tonight?"

Amused, I smirk, "You know me better than that, Mom."

"I know that of all of your brothers you are the least likely to punch someone who hasn't hit you first, Jaxson. *That's* what I know." She cocks her hip out to lean against the counter with me. "So what I'm wondering is…what are you up to?"

"You really think I'm going to tell you?" I smirk.

Her smile grows. "No. I don't."

"That's my girl."

"I wish I had some. You boys are a mystery to me, most days."

"You raised us to be like that."

Her brown eyes twinkle with mischief. "Indeed I did. No pussies in our family."

Laughing, I kiss her cheek and tell her, "I'll be back later."

7

JAXSON

Tapping my Jeep's steering wheel I stare at the large two-story American Foursquare house set deep inside a well-landscaped lawn.

I've watched a feminine-shaped, gracefully moving silhouette pass one of the second-story windows enough times to indicate she's alone, and she's pacing.

What's going on up there?

Is it Rachel?

It could be her mother. Can't be sure because gauzy curtains are in my way.

The lights shut off downstairs a half-hour ago.

I've been biding my time.

I'm a patient man most days.

Working a ranch will do that to a man, but I was also

born with a natural calm in my bones, so this itchy impatience is an anomaly.

What I want to know is, where is the douche bag?

I haven't seen a man's silhouette pass that window once. If it were Ellen Sawyer's room, then John would be there, too, I reckon.

Is it possible that Rachel and her boyfriend aren't allowed to stay in the same room while they're visiting?

Fuck, I don't even know if she's staying here or if she moved back to Atlanta, too.

She could be in a whole different neighborhood.

John Sawyer could be sleeping in the chair downstairs and that's Ellen pissed that he's been drinking.

I'm making up possibilities.

I have no idea if he even drinks.

Am I really going to chance this?

Fuck it.

Stepping out of my Jeep my boots hit the cement hard, and I head toward the house.

Only four cars have driven by since I got here.

It's a quiet street, but I scan it for anyone who might see me, feeling the old adrenaline charge into my blood like I'm a kid trying to get Rachel to sneak out to go to the park with me like I did about a hundred times.

* * *

"Jaxson, there are snakes here!" she whispered, ten years old and cute as hell since her silver braces got put in. She was always hiding them, trying not to smile. It made making her show 'em a game.

"So you better stay close to me," I whispered, pushing the low-hanging live oak branches out of the way so we could get through.

I never liked to stay on the cut grass portion of the park near our home. The forest that framed it was a better adventure. Mostly because there really were snakes.

But I wouldn't tell her we were there because I hoped to catch one.

She would never have come with me.

"Oh, like you can save me from a snake," she threw at my back as we trudged along.

I proudly announced, "I could kill fifty pythons!"

Her bright blue eyes rolled. "Yeah, right." But she came with me anyway.

For a good distance we wordlessly crunched through dead leaves and living ivy vines, avoiding Spanish moss and the skin-digging chiggers that hid inside them.

She lucked out that night.

I didn't.

Not one snake slithered by.

I felt totally jipped.

The thing was I wanted to impress her by catching one but since that wasn't going to happen I decided to climb the winding, centuries old branches of an oak tree instead.

"Come on!" I waved her up.

Muttering loads of objections Rachel followed, grabbing knots in the wood to pull herself up with. I walked along the thickest, horizontal branch as though it were a balance beam. She was right behind me but way less confident, so she slipped. I grabbed her arm just in time to steady her. "Whoa now!" Her legs shook and we both lowered our bodies to straddle the branch, facing each other, legs swinging below.

"I wasn't really going to fall," Rachel lied.

"You were."

"I wasn't."

"Yeah, you were."

"I wasn't!!!" Her eyes flashed and I dropped it.

For a whole second.

"You were."

"Jaxson!"

Laughing, I pulled off some bark and tossed it as far as I could as though I were skipping rocks on a docile stream. She started to do the same, but her fingers faltered. I glanced over and saw she was staring down at the tree, not happy.

"I was just messing with you, Rachel," I said, thinking she was mad at me.

I secretly hated when she was mad at me, even though I needled her any chance I could get.

With her eyes locked on the resistant piece of bark she listlessly told me, "We're moving away, Jaxson."

I blinked and stared at her for a long moment. "Where?"

"New York. My dad got a job there."

I pulled off a larger piece and there was a sinking in my stomach as I tossed it. "That's far away."

Her eyes rose to meet mine. "Yeah."

She and I picked at the bark for a long time while cicadas chirped unseen in the darkness. I sat on that branch with Rachel Sawyer feeling like something bad was happening but there was nothing I could do about it.

"We should go."

"Okay," she unhappily whispered. Sniffling, she looked at me and asked, "Will you help me down, Jaxson?"

She'd never asked for help before and it made her leaving feel real. "Sure," I whispered, my mind on a future without Rachel.

8

RACHEL

I can't stop fidgeting. Even reading a book on my Kindle didn't calm me down. I couldn't focus on the story and that never happens to me. Ever. Books are my escape. I lean into them with the relief of an athlete after a hard game when they soak their aching muscles and let the battle wash off their souls.

But for me the battle is simply day-to-day life.

Books can usually make all my troubles disappear, except when my boyfriend ends things, leaving me to sweep up the ashes while my parents watched. What a nightmare that was.

* * *

"I'm sorry, Ellen. I was really looking forward to this weekend of getting to know you." he'd lied when I followed him downstairs to

meekly watch him catch his Lyft. "But this case my firm is working on just took a turn for the worse and I have to get back."

He left the rest to their imaginations.

Which of course as soon as his taillights vanished twisted it into, "He works too hard, Rachel. He's like your father was. And you know that nearly ruined us."

"Now Ellen," Dad defended, his voice harsh.

"John, remember Tanya?"

He shut up at the reminder of the mistress who almost broke my parent's marriage into bloody pieces, eight years ago. Then Mom turned back to me.

"When you're young you think work is sooooo important, but Rachel honey, take my life experience for every drop of gold it's worth. Life is about the time spent together. That's what matters!"

* * *

Deciding to drown this anxiety with attempted sleep I pull the comforter back, forgetting I'm still in my dress.

A pebble hits my window.

I straighten up like a shot and drop the blanket.

I haven't heard that sound since I was a kid.

"No," I whisper. "It can't be."

My heart beats faster as I wait for the rest of a coded signal Jaxson and I thought up at age eight, one I'd completely forgotten about until now.

Two more pebbles hit the glass, one after the other.

55

My hand floats up to parted lips as I stare at the gauzy curtain. "Okay, that can't be a coincidence."

Three more pebbles hit it.

That's it. Our signal.

Gasping, I rush to look.

A mirage is staring up at me, work boots firmly planted on my parent's lawn. I've seen that head craned up so many times, but in a smaller face with boyish features. Long gone, they've been replaced with a grown man's rugged stubble, sharp lines and eyes that have seen hardship and joys I've been left out of.

I yank the window up, a gust of wind lifting my hair. Silently I mouth, "How did you know I was here?!"

He mouths back, slowly, so I can read his lips, "Is the douche bag with you?"

On a stifled smile I hesitate, then shake my head.

He waves me down, mouthing, "Come on!"

Come on...

Just like he always used to say.

Slipping my heels back on, I swear under my breath, and then past the quiet of my parent's bedroom and down the stairs I tiptoe.

Just like I always used to do.

Suddenly I'm no longer thirty-two.

I'm eight, nine and ten.

And I could get grounded.

Ever so slowly I close the front door behind me and turn to find him waiting, dangerously close to me.

Seeing Jaxson Cocker standing here so tall on my parent's new porch in a house I've never slept in until this weekend, feels incredibly strange and familiar.

His deep voice takes me again by surprise as he asks in his lowest volume, "They didn't want you staying in the same room?"

"He went back to New York. We...had a fight."

"Did you punch him, too?"

I can't help but smile. "No."

Jaxson blinks to my lips. "All bark no bite, that's always been you."

"What are you doing here, Jaxson?"

Without warning, he takes me by the arm. I'm expecting him to guide me to the small park just up the road like the old days, but instead he stops on the lawn an audibly safer distance from the house, and asks me in the strangest voice, "Do you love him?"

Stunned, my lips slowly part. "That's a very direct question."

"Yes or no."

Never leaving his eyes, I whisper a true, "Yes."

He huffs, lips tight. "So you won't come with me."

"To the park?"

"To my house."

I whisper, "To your house?" shocked.

That's a much deeper invitation than sneaking off as children, platonic because you're too young to be anything else.

We're both thirty-two now.

Jaxson Cocker was always terribly cute when he was a boy, but he has grown into the type of man who has undoubtedly had dozens of women in his bed who never tell him no, which is what I'm thinking as jealousy flies into my veins from out of nowhere.

"To your house," I repeat like I want to make sure I heard him right.

"Yes. Now." He's staring at me like the answer should be obvious.

"You're very sure of yourself," I mutter.

"What?" he frowns. "No, I just want to see you. Spend a little time with you. See how you've been."

From the chemistry crackling between our bodies I know that's a load of crap. And even though I know this, I have this crazy urge to throw myself into his arms. It's killing me that the two feet of distance between us feels way too far.

"Oh Jaxson…" I cover my face with both hands, aching to say yes. He says nothing, waiting for me to decide on my own what I want.

If I go to his house, we won't be just talking.

It's all over his face and the way his muscles are tense like he wants to pounce on me right now. Like he's struggling against the same urge I am.

My body is screaming to accept him in.

His bedroom eyes are impossible to deny.

I can't do this.

I think we should take a break…

"I shouldn't."

"No, you shouldn't," Jaxson grimly agrees. "And I shouldn't be asking you."

"As if that's ever stopped you," I mutter to the lawn.

He reaches out and lifts my chin, forcing me to look at him again. "Rachel. Why did I run into you?"

"I don't know!"

With calloused fingers holding me steady, he stares into my eyes like he's about to kiss me come hell or high water.

I try to object.

I open my mouth to speak.

No words come out.

Jaxson leans in so close that the sexy heat of his breath brushes my lips.

"How did you leave it?"

"Oh God, Jaxson, I can't."

"How?"

"We're…taking a break."

"Come on." He takes my hand, leading my reluctant heels hobbling on the grass toward a black Jeep parked ahead.

Come on. Come on. Come on.

Those two words dictated the favorite memories of my childhood.

They made me feel special that Jaxson, the boy who needed no one, wanted to spend his free time with me.

I also got into more trouble following those two words than any little girl should.

But I'm not a child anymore. I can resist Jaxson Cocker if I try.

I tug away from his hold, feeling a chill rush into my arm at the loss of his touch. Ignoring the unexpected sensation I set my jaw firm and tell him, "I can't."

We stand here at the edge on the front lawn, staring at each other like we wish we were naked. I've never felt this type of chemistry before.

Jaxson takes a step closer.

I take one back.

He rakes fingers through his thick sandy-brown hair and cuts an angry look to me.

No, it's not angry.

It's desperate.

"Do you think this is a coincidence, Rachel? You coming to that market today? My being there?"

"I..."

"Because I wasn't supposed to be there! I'm part of a co-op. That cheese originates from my farm but I don't make it. I sell the milk to other people who do, and they sell it at markets. I was helping out a sick friend today."

Embarrassed about Ryan, I overlap his speech, stammering to explain, "—If you're trying to defend yourself because he called you a loser, please stop! He only said that because he saw something between us, whatever *this* is." I motion in the air from his body to mine. "I know you're not a loser, Jaxson! There's nothing wrong with hard work."

I gasp as he closes the distance, his voice becoming deeper as he looms over me, looking absolutely gorgeous. "I punched him because when it comes to that douche bag, I am the loser."

"Jaxson—"

"—Not because of what I'm doing with my life, but because he has you." Off my shock, his voice shifts. "Rachel, I don't work those things unless I have to. I hate crowds. I wasn't meant to be there! Or maybe I was. I'm not going to talk you into anything. I don't even know what I'm doing here. This can only end badly." Pulling out his keys Jaxson heads for his Jeep with his face contorted like he can't believe he just said all that. His back is tense under the denim shirt and his hands are fists.

As I watch him go my heart tears into two distinct shards – one half that's committed to a man in New York City, the other half walking across a quiet road in Georgia, never to be seen again if I walk away.

Holding my breath the ache grows stronger, but I turn and head back to the porch. He's right. It can only end in tears.

Get in the house, Rachel.

Keep walking.

I wasn't meant to be there.

I hear the Jeep fire up and glance over my shoulder.

Revving the engine from the driver's seat Jaxson looks tortured as he mouths, "Come on."

I shake my head and continue to the sensible choice.

The rumble of the Jeep must have woken my mom, because their upstairs window jerks open and out thrusts her confused face.

I wasn't meant to be there.

His wheels squeal off the curb.

She and I lock surprised gazes. She spots the Jeep and her eyes narrow then shift back to meet mine.

Or maybe I was…

An explosion in my bloodstream spins me around to sprint faster than I ever have in my life. "Jaxson! Wait! Stop!!"

The running lights enflame bright red as he hits the brakes.

My mother shouts into the quiet of the night. "Rachel! Where are you going?!!"

I make it to his hood and lay my hands on it holding his eyes for a quick beat through the windshield before yelling to my mother, "Jaxson Cocker is a bad influence, Mom!"

Hanging out the window so far she might fall out, she yells at the top of her lungs, "NO, RACHEL, DON'T!"

But she's too late.

I jump in the passenger seat.

He's flooring the gas before the door's even closed.

The tires squeal triumph down the street as jasmine-scented wind whips through my hair.

If this is a mistake, I'm making it.

9

RACHEL

With our windows rolled down Jaxson and I drive over an hour, our silence charged with chemistry and consequences.

Here I wanted a proposal this weekend.

If Ryan had proposed on Friday, this wouldn't be happening.

Would it?

I can't say for sure that it would have stopped me, and that is deeply disturbing. This man to my left has a connection with me I've never been able to deny, and my sitting beside him right now after my mother was screaming for me not to go, is a testament.

I glance over to the grown Jaxson Cocker beside me, seeing him as he was then, and also who he's become. He owns a farm? He has cows? I guess that solitary, rural lifestyle makes sense knowing what a loner he always was.

He only ever spent time with Jerald or I when we were children. The other boys at the school would have loved to have him as a friend. He was popular without a posse because he didn't want one. He ignored kids who didn't interest him, which was everyone outside of his brothers...and me.

He never needed much to keep him happy back then. Sometimes just the quiet and other times outdoor adventures. And maybe pissing a few people off along the way.

Which might be the reason I'm here now that I think about it.

Jaxson hated Ryan on sight, standing for everything Jaxson isn't, very much like how the teachers at our elite elementary school were. Buckhead is the ritziest neighborhood in Atlanta and our teachers were upper class and encouraged us to behave the same way.

Jaxson was never impressed with material things or status symbols.

And there Ryan was this morning wearing expensive everything, his hair fucking perfect, his shave close, calling Jaxson a loser.

Clean, upscale snob meets rough, ready to fight, tattooed cowboy.

Pissing Ryan off by absconding with his girlfriend is

exactly the type of thing Jaxson would enjoy.

Feeling my curious gaze resting on him Jaxson looks over to hold my look before turning back to the road with his strong, stubble-covered jaw clenching and unclenching. Just like my stomach.

I turn my focus to the window but there is only darkness outside.

After a while, he reaches over and touches my leg, then withdraws his hand and rests it on his own lap like he's struggling with this, too.

As I see his hand form a fist suddenly it settles into me that he's not doing this to get back at my boyfriend, just for sport. He's doing it because he has feelings for me.

"Are you as freaked out as I am," I whisper, wondering if I'm right.

He frowns and murmurs, "Yes," as the Jeep turns left onto a long driveway.

The air crackles between us and I shiver with apprehension, scanning the pitch-black night until I make out an old two-story barn up ahead. To the right of it is a long one-level structure, separated by at least twenty feet, but I'm not good with distance. Could be longer. I squint at it and finally give up trying to figure out why, from the looks of it, he has two barns. Fences extend far in both directions and it's impossible to see what is out there. The long driveway becomes bumpy as gravel replaces cement, punctured with jarring potholes created over time by the infamously unpredictable and dramatic Georgia storms.

The wheels come to a halt and dust fogs the air around us.

If Ryan saw this place, he'd laugh his ass off. And if I didn't know Jaxson from childhood I'd be scared shitless right now.

"Wait there," Jaxson says as I go for the handle. He comes around and opens my door, helping me down. When my heels are securely on uneven ground he still hasn't let go of my hand. "Remember the oak tree that last night?" he asks.

Staring into his eyes and knowing now I'm right about him caring for me, I whisper my answer, "Of course."

Jaxson nods satisfied he's not the only one who remembers the night I told him we were moving. He heads for the two-story barn. As I follow him, I'm surprised to find gorgeous patio furniture tucked invitingly into an enclosed porch there. Behind them large glass windows on either side of the front door span the entire structure. They're modern and almost floor to ceiling.

It's dark inside them so I can't see anything else yet, but I'm beginning to believe this isn't a barn after all, at least not anymore.

He picks out the right key then looks over his broad shoulder. "I can't believe I'm looking at you."

Without waiting for my response he lets us inside and my breath hitches with surprise at the sight. My eyebrows rise up as I walk around and take in all the little details of his home.

This first level is a large, high-ceilinged, open space with a living room to the right and kitchen to the far left. Two things separate them, a gorgeous iron and wood kitchen that houses a stove and oven, with silver pots hanging over it.

In the other direction an enormous steel and stone fireplace in front of a masculine, comfortable couch and worn dark chocolate leather chairs.

To the left where the kitchen ends are stairs leading to the second story. Under it, beside the kitchen is a guest bathroom he motions to, asking if I need to use it.

"I'm fine."

Square grey-brown wood beams are strategically placed throughout the lower floor. And now I know why the windows are so tall and run the entire front and south walls – they're to enjoy the view of his property during daylight.

A gorgeous dining table with heavy chairs on one side and a bench on the other is placed in the far corner, most likely to bask in the beauty when he starts his day.

Everything is rustic in style but I know quality and this

unique home is laden with it.

Jaxson is at the fireplace, shoulders tight. Kneeling down, his shirt tightens across his back muscles as he twists to look at me when I cross to one of the exposed beams. Touching it, I ask, "Is this reclaimed wood?"

"You have a good eye."

"Did you do all this yourself?"

Knotting newspaper sheets into kindling and staggering them over a thin layer of ash, he explains, "I designed it. Some men helped build it. And yes, I worked with them until it was finished."

"It's beautiful, Jaxson."

"It is," he says as he glances to me one more time.

The primal glint in his eyes brings it to my attention that we are alone now.

Far away from anyone.

Our parents can't find us.

Ryan can't find me.

Holy crap. What am I doing here?

I swallow and rest my back against the square beam.

The undulation of his muscles as he shoves twigs under the grate and piles three logs in a triangle on top, mesmerizes me. I have an alarming reaction to that arm-tattoo. I know 'everyone's' getting them, but not in the circles I run in.

I can't help but imagine him without that shirt because his body is incredible and I am a grown woman after all. Those sinewy forearms flexing as he works, his strong thighs adjusting his weight, the way his shirt tugs across his shoulders – all this has me in a spell where all I can think about is sex.

When we were children and he kissed me it was chaste and innocent. Sweet. But now we're adults. Neither of us is a virgin and from that cocky assuredness he carries in his natural gait, I know the grown up Jaxson Cocker is not the least bit insecure in the bedroom.

Pulling a long match from a metal box he flicks it off the iron, waiting for the tiny twigs to ignite as he touches the flame to them. Satisfied it will be enough to catch the wood, he tosses the match on top.

My heart races as he stands up and with his back still to me, runs his hands through his hair. His ass and large back are so perfect I bite my lip as heat pools between my thighs.

He slowly turns around to take me in. There's a bulge in his jeans now and by the determined look on his face he knows I see it. He crosses his arms making no excuses for it, and his deep green eyes take a hungry stroll down my body and then right back up.

Thickly he calls me out. "You're nervous."

"Nope."

That familiar smirk appears. "Yes you are."

"Well, let's talk about something then!"

An amused smile flashes as he shifts his legs out a little wider. My eyes flick to his crotch and back up, an action he doesn't miss. "How've you been, Rachel?"

I make what sounds like a strangled laugh. "For the past two decades? I've been good. Yeah, no complaints."

"Still can't believe you're in my house."

Alone in your house. And you're so fucking stunning I can hardly look at you.

I choke, "So…how have *you* been, Jaxson?"

"Really good. I'm happy." He's staring at me like he wants to stop talking.

Suddenly it feels like I've never been with a man. Like this is my first time or something. I feel like a kid again, like I might start giggling if he tries to kiss me and hoping to God he does.

I mutter, "That's great. I'm glad you're doing well."

He starts walking toward me and my breath hitches as his eyes darken with lust.

I push my back further into the beam and whisper, "Oh God, Jaxson? Now what do we do?"

"What do you *want* to do, Rachel?"

And there's that fucking smirk again. Hot damn.

71

10

RACHEL

On a quiet moan I beg him, "Don't ask me that. I don't know what I want."

Lie. Lie. Lie.

But we all need to lie to ourselves a little, sometimes, don't we?

Jaxson cocks his gorgeous head to hold my attention. "Rachel, I need you going into this with open eyes."

"What about you? Are yours closed?"

He shakes his head just once and as he thinks of how to answer that, glances to the side and licks his lips. I want those on me right now even though I suspect if I were a better woman I should be on a flight to New York to try and mend things with my boyfriend.

The boyfriend who told me he wanted a break.

Then lied to my mother so he could start it right away.

After I asked him not to go.

"Jaxson," I murmur, wanting to hear his answer. "Are you aware this is a disaster waiting to happen?"

"Yes, I am." He cuts a quick glance to my parted lips. "I know you love him. And I can tell by your expensive dress and hot-as-fuck heels that you're a city girl now. That means you don't belong here. I also know that I have to kiss you and I don't give a damn about what comes later."

He's on me, crushing me in a kiss so thrilling my knees start to buckle. His arm slips around me fast, and he holds me up as his jaw unlocks mine. Our tongues touch for the very first time.

The kiss becomes desperate until we're careening across the room to slam into a wall. We don't come up for air for a very long time.

He pulls away, catching his breath to stare at me a second with a stunned look on his face. I feel exactly the same way. But I'm here now and I'm not turning back.

To show him, I throw my arms above my head, holding his eyes while in this most submissive stance.

Jaxson groans and runs rough hands down my willing body, watching their travel down. He brushes his lips against mine then shakes his head a little. Moistened lips whisper down my panting neck as he grips my ass and pulls me against his stiff bulge. On impact he growls into my collarbone.

Our mouths lock again, moving and sculpting slowly, then fast, then slow again. As we kiss he pins my arms higher and grinds into me, sending an ache into me I've never felt.

With his knee and one hand he hikes the skirt of my dress up so that my panties become exposed. I feel the air warmed by the flickering flames and that heat reaches up the highest points of my thighs. I can tell he's hung like a beast.

It feels so good I want to cry, or scream, or tear him to shreds.

"Come on," he growls, lifting me up so that I'm straddling his hips as he carries me closer to the fireplace, kissing me the whole way. As he stands me up my legs are like wet noodles. Leaving me for the staircase, he looks over his shoulder and shakes his head like he can't believe how badly he wants me.

He growls, "Stay here," before he disappears upstairs.

Waiting I run a hand over my messy hair, my skirt still around my waist. I almost tug it down but decide I like it the way it is.

Reappearing a moment later with a white sheep-fur rug, Jaxson brings it over to lay before the fire. His eyes lock onto my silk and very wet panties. He licks his lips and my pussy clenches in response, begging for his touch.

Jaxson pulls me to lie on the rug, kneeling before me as my hair splays out. He's watching my face as he rubs my pussy through the moistened fabric. I'm moaning and boneless as he caresses me with such skill it becomes obvious once more that I was right about him. The way he's touching me, he's gotten practice by being a talented lover for many women.

Many women.

Suddenly I'm jealous.

Like seeing-red jealous.

I am so inexplicably pissed and hurt that I rise up and slap him.

He freezes, staring at me, as shocked as I am.

My lips part.

His form a grim line.

"I'm sorry," I breathe. "You're so good at that and I know you learned it somewhere else. And I...I...hate it."

He's panting softly as the flames trace red-orange light along the side of his sharp features. I stop apologizing because my explanation sounds stupid and makes no sense. It's not like I was here and he chose them over me.

I'm the one who moved away.

I had no choice. I was just a kid.

But when that decision was made for me, I also lost my friend.

But haven't we always been more than friends?

"I'm sorry I hit you, Jaxson," I whisper.

He looks like he's going to get up and leave me lying here.

Instead, he grabs my shoulders then fists my hair and kisses me hard, craning me back to deepen the kiss as I claw at his chest, feeling all the hills and valleys of his muscles through the denim shirt. We slip to the floor and I'm half-fighting him off and half-pulling him closer. I've never been like this before. I want to hurt him and I want to hold him.

"Rachel. I know how you feel."

One of my thighs gets lifted and he hooks my foot around his ass, halfway up on his knees, pulling my butt off the ground as he grinds into me kissing me like crazy. Low moans escape our gasping lips.

I know how you feel.

I'm on the verge of tears. A deep frown creases his handsome features as he notices but I shake my head and whisper to him, "Just don't stop. Please, don't stop."

His nostrils flare on a decision and he pulls at my dress so violently it rips. I give his denim shirt a rough yank, and two buttons explode off it.

"Fuck, I can't get close enough to you," he growls, unsnapping his belt buckle as he lunges down and captures me in another amazing kiss.

I don't have time to see what's coming. I've felt it through his jeans, and now I'm going to feel it inside me before I even see it. He yanks my panties to the side and slides his cock into my wetness so quickly that I yelp at his size and dig my fingers into his back, my own sharply arching. A low moan tears out of my core as he stretches my inner walls quickly.

Jaxson groans and, gripping one of my thighs to pull me off the rug, drives his manhood in to the hilt. I yelp again.

"Am I hurting you?" he demands, his voice deep with lust.

"Don't you dare fucking stop."

"Whatever you say, Rach."

We're half on our sides and he starts grinding with long sure thrusts.

"You're so tight," he growls, reaching for my tongue with his, cock growing harder.

He starts fucking me like he's making up for lost time.

"Oh God!!" I scream as a burst of pleasure tears through me.

"So wet," he groans. "God, you're so fucking wet!"

He changes rhythm, pulling almost all the way out and then sliding back in so slowly and deeply that I start to writhe. "Jaxson," I whimper as my orgasm breaks and hums a steady beat.

Grunting through clenched teeth, Jaxson holds his own climax in check to fuck me in a way that deliberately stretches my orgasm into the most intense one of my life.

When after it wanes, I stare up at him, stunned and tingling all over.

He's smiling at me. "You're beautiful."

Speechless, my eyelashes flutter as Jaxson Cocker traces my lips with calloused fingertips. He slowly pulls out of me.

"No," I moan. "Don't go."

"Shhhh." He slips my panties down my legs. "We've made a mess of these." As he tosses them, I glance down. My eyes literally go wide.

I felt it. Oh boy did I feel it.

But seeing his gorgeous cock is an altogether more compelling experience.

He is fucking enormous, wet and glittering in the firelight.

Staring at it, I whisper, "You're beautiful, too."

Jaxson chuckles and bends to kiss his way up to my stomach, starting at my calves and slowly traveling. He takes my breasts in both hands and massages one while kissing and tonguing the other, his erect cock against my leg. My back arches on a moan as he arouses my nipples into painfully sharp points.

He sits back on his knees to slowly spread my legs so he can take a good long look at my naked, wet pussy. "Looks as good as she feels," he smiles, dipping down to have a lick. "Slippery, tight little pussy," he growls into my sensitive folds.

I whisper in awe, "Dirty talk," because I never hear dirty talk and I'm surprised how much I like it.

As his tongue sharpens and flicks my clit like they should teach at colleges across America, I cry out and moan like I have never moaned before.

He's found the right spot and pays it close attention, driving me to the point of madness until I scream, "I need you inside me! Please fuck me! I need it!"

He yanks me by my hips straight onto his cock without so much as a warning, filling and stretching me so quickly I gasp. He groans low and guttural as his head falls back under the pleasure as he pumps between my thighs. The veins are pulsing wildly on his thick neck, tattoos rippling on his chest and down his left arm.

I claw my way up his body, straddling his lap like I've just woken up for the first time.

I grab the back of Jaxson's head and kiss him hard, our open lips careening into each other without shame. As we bite and lick each other he starts fucking me rougher and faster. I ride him like this until he roars. His girth fills to its fullest right before he shouts, "Holy fucking hell!" and explodes, his orgasm so primal I find myself falling over the cliff too, joining him, moaning into each other's panting lips as we cum together.

When he lays us back down he easily stays inside me. Lazily sliding his hand over my hip, he pauses because the nearby fire was a little too hot against my bare skin.

"Here," he murmurs, pulling the soft rug up against my reddened hip. "I didn't know you were overheating."

"Didn't you?" I smile.

He laughs into my neck and presses slow caressing kisses there for a deliciously long time.

11

JAXSON

At the distant crow of Hank, I wake in bed, blinking the lack of sleep away. I got maybe an hour. The blanket is covering Rachel. Even her creamy shoulders are hidden. Her hair is wavy from the shower we took together after a couple more rounds of reacquainting ourselves. The shower saw more action than it has in a couple years, too.

But it's Sunday now, isn't it?

Back to him.

My time with her is soon over.

In the stable I get relief from obsessing about this mess I've put myself in, with the familiar rituals I do every day of my life. Each of my twenty-two cows gets attached to the milking parlor, a row of machines designed to make this process time-efficient and easy for all involved. Starting at

81

one end of the row, with the first cow done, I strain the warm white liquid into a stainless steel bucket and bring it to the milk tank where it stays at the correct cooled temperature until the guys pick it up for turning into whatever they like.

Connie moos loudly as I go to let them out.

Smiling, I walk over.

"Hey Con, did I almost forget to pet you? My mind is elsewhere, girl. My apologies." Stroking her thick neck until she calms down, I comfort her with promises of good weather. "You ready for some sunlight? Looks clear today."

She vocalizes her approval, the most social of my girls.

Strolling to the gate, I crack it open so they have to exit in single file where I can touch each one as they amble past me into the golden grey light of morning to graze on the three-hundred and forty acres I bought on a loan right out of college. When my grandfather passed he left all of us boys enough that I was able to pay that off.

I always wanted this life.

It's a lot of work running a healthy farm, but it's soul soothing for a man like me.

Lots of quiet. Lots of hands-on labor.

It's the reason I was in shape enough to go all night with Rachel, since gyms bore the shit out of me.

Rachel.

Shading my eyes as I gaze west, I try to see her walking

around through my bedroom window. She's probably still dreaming.

I don't know what's about to happen, especially since I'm not altogether clear on what I want. Never planned this.

In Georgia you have screen doors because the bugs'll try and fly away with you if you give them a chance. I've got two screens, one for the enclosed patio, the other for my house, which I have to get fixed. Missing the lever that is supposed to keep it from slamming, it hits the doorframe hard behind me.

With the noise having woken her, Rachel calls down in a sleepy voice from the bedroom, "Jaxson?"

"I'm here!" I reassure her. "I'm just gonna make some coffee."

She calls down, voice losing steam, "Not yet. Come back."

"Be right up."

Washing my hands in the kitchen sink, I turn and set my cowboy hat on an antique, bare-wood chair. Staring out the window for about five minutes I obsess all over again about what comes next with us.

Fucking New York City of all places.

I decide to wait on coffee and take advantage of what little time I have left.

Taking the stairs two at a time, I find her back asleep.

Her naked body is shifted toward me now. The blanket has slipped down, exposing a breast held softly by gravity. Her pink lips are open and as I watch her lightly snoring I cross my arms over my white tank, old jeans hanging low without the belt.

She looks like a fuckin' angel, that's the problem.

Tearing off my clothes I climb in with her.

She mews like a cat as my naked body enfolds hers.

She smells like my pine-scented soap, but her own smell is mixed in. Inhaling deeply, I close my eyes and swear inwardly that I am not ready for these feelings, especially not under the circumstances.

Maybe not ever.

Half in dreamland Rachel Sawyer presses her ass into me and murmurs something unintelligible. My cock has chosen to ignore my mind's reservations. It only remembers the four times it was inside her. She moans, as my erection grows more urgent.

"I know you're sore," I moan into her shoulder.

"You feel amazing, Jaxson. I'll warm up. Don't stop."

Those words are an aphrodisiac to any man, but to me they're a dissolving of my doubts, at least for the time being.

I flip her onto her stomach and slip my fingers slowly into her cunt until I get her wet and moaning with desire for more, angling her so that I can get in deep.

Slipping my cock inch-by-inch into her slippery pussy, Rachel writhes, moving like she knows what I like to see – a woman who loves what I feel like and how I move.

She grabs onto the hand that's gripping her hip, her elbow bent high. Her fingers trap mine there and I squeeze back as I thrust slowly, loving the gorgeous view of her body.

She grabs onto my headboard and I keep moving slow and steady, knowing she's sore, until her body gives in to me completely.

She cries out as we cum together. "Holy shit," I moan as the pulses rack through our bodies.

We've done that all four times last night, even the shower. It's taken me to a whole new level of confusion at how I'm going to be able to let her go. It's not that sex is everything, it's that this kind of connection isn't common. I've never felt it before.

I'm good in bed. Anyone I've been with will tell you that.

Mostly, because I love it. All of it.

But simultaneous orgasms are not an 'every time' thing. Especially not the first night you're with someone. Not unless something greater than just sex is going on. I feel that with her. There's an energy between us that is tearing me apart and putting me back together.

In the aftermath of this slow morning fuck we kiss for

a long time until suddenly her smile fades.

"I have to call my mom."

"I know. Mine texted me already."

Rachel makes a face. "Are you serious?"

"She thought I was going to stay the night in Atlanta. So did I."

Laughing, Rachel asks, "So…you got us in trouble with our parents is what you're saying?"

Stroking her naked body as I remain inside her, I say on a low laugh, "Yep. Guess no T.V. for a week."

"Oh please! You never got in trouble. That was always me!"

"Parents are more lenient with boys."

Rachel stares at my smile and reaches up to touch my nose. "I like how you've grown up."

Like I'm going to say something sweet I lean in to whisper in her ear, "When did the braces come off, Jaws?"

She hoots at my reference to the bad guy in James Bond's *Moonraker*. "You used to call me that! I forgot. That was so mean!"

Staring down into her smiling face, I ask the question that's been gnawing at me, "When's your flight?"

Her smile falters as she blinks at me. "You knew I was leaving today?"

"I do now." I push a lock of sandy-brown hair from

her forehead, tracing her skin. "What do you do there, Rachel? For a living."

"I'm a writer," she whispers. "Editorials for blogs and newspapers. I have a few non-fiction books out about travel, too."

My eyebrows go up. "You're a travel writer?"

"Restaurants, hidden places, but mostly I like to write about the people I meet, the quirky differences that make each place unique."

We stare at each other and I know she's thinking the same thing I am. We both know there isn't much to write about where I live.

"Nice. They send you to these places you travel to?"

"My publisher does for the books. That's how I eventually got to be paid for blogging when most aren't. And I researched successful bloggers early on, building my own core audience until..." she trails off and shrugs her shoulders, misreading my expression for disinterest.

What she's really seeing, I won't tell her. "That's good. I'd like to read some of your stuff."

She searches my face. "I should go."

"Rachel, I'm not sorry we did this."

Something familiar is in her eyes, not from childhood but from other women I've been with.

She wants me to ask her to stay.

It's occurred to me.

No…it's haunted me ever since I first kissed her last night, and felt something I never had before.

But what could she achieve here? Interview my cows and give up everything she's built in one of the greatest cities in the world? And by greatest, I mean size and impact.

I've been to New York, stopped off on my way to visit Justin when he was at Yale.

I saw the appeal, but only to visit.

Not a fan.

I'm a country boy blood and bone. Maybe that's why this is so compelling – she's so different from me. But I know deep down that's not really why. Hell, I knew it all the way back when we were kids.

* * *

As usual Mrs. Connolly shouted at recess, "Jerald and Jaxson Cocker! Get over here! Now!" We stopped chasing Cora and Heather and hit each other on the shoulder, laughing as we made our way back to enjoy our daily scolding.

"They called Jerald 'cute,' Mrs. Connolly, and you know that's a lie," I explained as my younger brother snickered beside me. I was nine. He was seven, but just an inch shorter. He was my best friend and followed me everywhere, trying his best to think of ways to outdo me.

She wasn't amused. "How many times are you going to have to hear from me 'no chasing girls!' before I send you home?"

Jerald whispered, "Ten-thousand."

"I heard that!"

Behind her I saw something I wasn't expecting and my face changed. Rachel Sawyer has just walked out of the library with her arms full of books and her hair curled for picture day. It was normally bone straight.

I stood a little straighter because while we were friends and played after school, I noticed her that day for the first time as a girl, and not a gross-girls-are-stupid creature.

Mrs. Connolly was yammering on about whatever and I nodded like I was listening, but Rachel had just tucked a little of her curled hair behind her ear after a breeze misplaced it. As she did that simple gesture, she glanced over and caught me staring.

She froze.

I walked away from the teacher.

"Jaxson! Where are you going?"

"Sorry, Mrs. Connolly," I muttered, glancing back over my shoulder. "Rachel's books are heavy."

The teacher's mouth dropped in surprise. Jerald watched me, blonde eyebrows contorted with confusion.

Why would I help a girl with her books, they both wordlessly asked.

I continued on my journey.

Rachel was staring at me like there was no one else around.

I walked up and knocked the books out of her hands. "Oops!"

"Jaxson Cocker!!" Rachel shouted, and I took off running. She chased me. My brother laughed long and hard.

I got in trouble that day, but I don't remember the punishment.

I only remember Rachel Sawyer's bright blue eyes locked on me and only me.

12

RACHEL

"Is Dad home?" I whisper as I take my shoes off in the immaculate foyer of my parent's new house. Mom says wearing shoes inside brings negative energy into your home. I think it's really from habit of keeping the New York dirt manageable.

"No, thank God."

Sighing, I lock eyes with her. "Okay, let's have it."

"Did you sleep with him!?"

"Mom!"

She's practically spitting she's so upset. "Jaxson Cocker. I can't believe you." And as though she's fumbling for what to say, she shouts, "He always got you in trouble! Nice to know things haven't changed!"

Throwing her arms in the air, Mom flips around for

the kitchen where she will no doubt salve her nerves with a Sunday morning mimosa. "This is the worst thing that's ever happened!" she mutters to herself.

It sounds like she believes that. Which is a bit of an overreaction in my opinion.

But we are church-going folk. At least, she still is. I've kinda slipped off the pious wagon. I still pray almost every night, and that keeps my Catholic guilt at bay. I've got bigger things to worry about now, though, don't I? And Mom's apparently not going to make it easier on me.

I take a deep breath of patience and follow her. There is no avoiding this mess. "First you don't like Ryan, and now you don't like Jaxson."

"I *never* liked Jaxson, Rachel. You know that!" She whips open her brand new refrigerator and pulls out an unopened bottle of champagne, reaching in for fresh squeezed orange juice predictably after. Casting a look at my expression, she mutters, "Don't ride me about this. It's the only morning I drink and you know that! And I went to church today, praying for you!" Her slippers shuffle to the cabinet for a glass.

"Grab two," I quietly say.

She glances over the shoulder of her comfy housedress and raises her eyebrows.

"Mom, if we're going to have this conversation, then I

need a drink."

"Did you sleep with him!?!!"

I gape at her, then shut my mouth. "No."

She huffs back like she doesn't believe me, "Rachel, I'm serious. This is very important. Did you?!"

Stunned and ashamed, I whisper, "No, mom. We just talked." To sell my lie, I add, "We kissed. That's it."

Shaking her head she hands me the champagne like she doesn't trust herself not to drop the bottle. I'm no first-timer so when I pop the cork, only a tiny mist drifts out, no overflow.

As soon as we have mimosas in hand, she mutters under her breath before a very large sip, "I saw him a few weeks ago. Knew it was him right off the bat. That Cocker swagger. He also looked dirty. Like he's got no money. Stay away from him."

Smiling at her ignorance and superiority, I gently defend him, "He's a cowboy, mom. He has a gorgeous ranch that's over three-hundred acres."

The formidable Ellen Sawyer stares at me a beat then resumes her tirade. "Well, he's not a lawyer, Rachel! And you know that while Ryan might be career-driven and egotistical, he will always be able to provide for you."

"What year are we living in?" I groan. "And you don't have to worry. Jaxson doesn't want anything more from me than…" She waits for me to say the rest, and because I lied to her, I pretend to act appalled, "…my body! He wanted more. I didn't give it to him because I couldn't do that to Ryan."

Oh my…I'm diving deeper into depravity.

Visibly relieved, she demands, "And what are you going to tell your boyfriend?"

"He's not really my boyfriend right now. We had a fight and he said he…"

"Rachel!"

Unable to defend my actions in front of one who's lived through more life experience than I have, who I respect very much, and who also knows me too well to believe it's over with me and Ryan, I can only sigh, "I'm going to tell him the truth."

"Don't you dare!"

Stunned I stare, mimosa suspended in front of my mouth. "What are you saying?"

She takes another gulp, blinking away to the window while struggling for words of wisdom. Finally, her shoulders slump and she whispers, "Rachel, telling someone you cheated only takes the burden off you and puts it on them. I know you didn't sleep with him, so what is there to tell? You're not going to see him again, are you?" She waits for my plans.

God, what a horrible feeling this is.

All I want is to see him again.

I shake my head. "No, I'm not seeing him again. It...didn't go well."

Except it did.

Waving her hand in conclusion, she says, "Then restrain yourself from putting that on Ryan *and* your relationship. I wasn't a fan of the man, Rachel, but you are. And he is very successful. He's only going to go up! Unless he's a lying, underhanded lawyer...is he?"

"What? No! He's one of the good guys, Mom."

Exhaling, she mutters from behind her slender flute glass, "Then don't say anything, for God's sake! It was a night of conversation and that's all. A ghost from your past sprung up and took a bite out of you. It's not going anywhere. It will never go anywhere. It can never go anywhere." She touches my heart, her blue eyes filled with meaning. "So it stays *here*. And this is where it never leaves."

I know she means the secret, but for me it hits differently. As much as I know it's time to go back to my normal life, Jaxson's taste is still on my tongue. His masculine scent haunts my senses as if he's standing right in front of me. The pressure of his hands is embedded into my psyche and I don't know if it will always be.

I already miss all of him.

She pulls back a shaking hand. "Understand?"

"Yes."

"Am I making sense to you?"

"Mom, don't be so scared. I didn't do anything. You don't have to worry."

I can do all the worrying for both of us.

She clinks her empty glass to mine. "Good."

There's something very personal about her response to what I've done – even though she now believes our childhood crush went unconsummated. I've never seen my mother shake, or drink this quickly. She enjoys her cocktails, but she has downed that thing like she was hoping there was cake at the bottom.

"Mom…did you ever cheat on dad?"

Her eyebrows fly up. "Me?" She shakes her head with finality. "Of course I didn't." But she's walking away before she completes her sentence. With my hand on the marble counter I didn't grow up with, and an almost full glass in my freshly trembling hand, I watch her carefully.

This had nothing to do with Jaxson.

The ghost from the past was her own guilt and shame, unhealed.

My church-going, self-righteous mother…just lied to me.

13

RACHEL

My key jams in the lock of our West Village apartment. I swear under my breath then gasp as the door opens revealing Ryan in well-fitting jeans and t-shirt, his dark hair wet from the shower. He must have gone to the gym right before my plane landed. If I'd have flown back here earlier, I might have had alone time to gather my wits. The yapping passenger next to me on the flight did nothing to settle my nerves.

His expression says he's been waiting for me, and knows we have to talk. "Hi Rach."

"Hey." I force a smile.

"Cab ride okay?"

Numbly I nod, still outside in the hall. "It was fine."

His quiet voice is deepened with sincerity. "I'm sorry, baby."

My eyes close for a brief second. "Me too."

On a half-smile, Ryan turns to let me see the apartment is overflowing with flowers. Dozen of sunflowers.

Shit.

"Your favorite, right?" he asks off my dazed look as if he's not sure he got it right.

"Yes," I whisper, struggling to believe what I'm seeing. "They're lovely."

Memories are peculiar, aren't they? They imprint you with likes and dislikes you often don't remember the origin of until it bites you in the ass. I'd forgotten why sunflowers were my favorite until I saw Jaxson's smirk after he punched Ryan, remembering that day at the abandoned factory for the first time in years.

These flowers don't stand for forgiveness and apology no matter what Ryan thinks. They stand for a first kiss I shared when I was only nine, one that impacted me in ways I am only beginning to understand.

And now they're everywhere, in the wrong home.

"Let me get that." Ryan takes my rolling suitcase, carrying it to our bedroom.

Walking to the largest bouquet I touch soft yellow petals, closing my eyes at the irony.

I'm a piece of shit.

"Ryan?"

"Yeah?"

I jump. "Oh! I didn't realize you were in the room."

"I was watching you. You don't like the flowers, or you don't like what happened last night."

Oh dear God.

Helping me out of my coat, he continues, "I shouldn't have jumped to that." Off my questioning look, he adds, "To taking a break so fast. I was pissed. Friday night with your parents was a —"

"—Blast," I dryly interrupt.

Chuckling, Ryan says, "Yeah. Loads of fun." As he turns to the coat rack I slip out of my painful heels. "And then that bullshit at the farmers market. I hadn't even had my coffee yet."

"Not a great start to a day," I smile, silently hiding my shame.

"And then suddenly I'm under the gun about marriage and I was just overwhelmed, babe. I snapped." Walking to me he places his hands on my hips and squeezes. "I spent all night thinking about it. Did you?"

"Umm…of course I did. I'm really thirsty, Rye. Mom made mimosas this morning and we got a little drunk."

Amused, he starts for our modern kitchen. "Bet the plane ride didn't help the dehydration, either."

"Yeah—"

"—I got wasted on the plane last night. I get it." He pours ice cold water for me as I lean against the kitchen counter we've prepped food on for over a year. This was our first place together and everything in it is mingled with memories I can't help reliving.

As he animatedly tells me about how, out of pure coincidence, he sat next to a couple of guys on the plane he knew from college, I sip the water and barely hear a word. Our relationship is playing out for me like it's a 3D movie on an IMAX screen.

I know human beings rationalize bad behavior, but I'm not lying to myself when I see all the things that showed how we'd drifted apart, now that I'm watching him talk. Maybe that's why I wanted to lock it down with an engagement ring, because I feared we were on a slow decline destined for failure.

But now here Ryan is acting like his old self, the man I was so attracted to. He's laughing and mimicking the flight attendant asking them to keep it down. Gone is the sulky irritability, the quickness to snap my head off.

And when I fake a laugh so well that Ryan thinks I'm totally on board and hearing everything he's told me, he takes me in his arms and kisses me.

"Hey," he murmurs against hesitant lips. "You're tense. You're still mad at me, aren't you?"

Resting my forehead to his, I whisper, "We haven't been us for a long time, Ryan."

His voice lowers. "I know. I've been working too much."

"It's not all you."

"It's mostly me," he says, dazzling me with one of those smiles I fell in love with.

I smile and slip my arms around his neck. "It was mostly you."

He chuckles then kisses me again. "Being here without you last night made me miss you."

Ouch.

Ouch.

Ouch.

I was doing things last night that had nothing to do with you, Ryan, and if you knew about them you would be yelling at me and probably calling me all kinds of names. What am I supposed to do with all these feelings? I have loved you for so long.

Instead of saying what is spinning in my head I murmur, "You sure you don't need more guy-time in your life? Sounds like that's what might have happened."

He shrugs. "I need more fun. That's what I need." Sliding his hands down to my ass, he smirks. "Ready for make-up sex?"

No fucking way.

"Oh honey, I'm tired. Can we do that another time?"

The playfulness fades as he nods, trying to hide his hurt. "Sure. I'm moving pretty fast after saying I wanted a break. I get it."

Sucking on my lips, I pull away. He follows me into our bedroom where I begin to unpack. A text from my phone sounds.

Oh no.

I glance to where my purse is hiding somewhere in the sunflower nightmare.

Ryan goes to get it – normally a very natural thing to do because we don't hide anything from each other. Not that I ever see his phone because it's always close to him. Mine? I leave it where I drop it.

But tonight is very different from every night for the past two plus years. I gave my number to Jaxson.

As Ryan reads the text I can't breathe.

His eyes slowly rise to meet mine as a deep frown cuts into his forehead.

My mouth gets instantly stuffed with a million saliva-sucking cotton balls.

Ryan starts back, eyes locked on me, frown deepening. He holds up the phone. "Your mom thinks I'm a jerk?" He hands it to me.

He may be a jerk, but he'll stick by you.

I swallow. "She's probably still drunk."

Shoving his hands in his pockets he watches as I keep unpacking.

"She'll grow to like you, Ryan. You weren't exactly the ideal houseguest."

Chuckling, "True," he heads to watch TV, smacking the top of the doorframe on his way out. "I can be a jerk sometimes. But she was no princess! Jesus, what are we gonna do with all these flowers?"

How about throwing them out the window before I wake up?

Would that raise any alarm bells?

Nah…not at all.

14

RACHEL

"I can't believe I was wrong!" Sylvia mutters, smoothing the black cloth napkin over her lap as the waiter walks away with our lunch order. "I really thought he was going to propose!"

She's usually right on the nose when it comes to affairs of the heart.

Sylvia predicted Ryan would ask me out the night two-and-a-half years ago when she and I enjoyed a few stiff martinis at Lois bar in the East Village before this handsome, dark-haired man strolled in wearing an expensive suit and a confident swagger like he owned the place.

She also predicted he'd suggest we move in together after the softball tournament between his law firm and their rivals.

And she predicted her own boyfriend would turn out to be gay.

All came true.

And of course now he's her ex-boyfriend.

"Not only were you wrong, he said he wanted a break."

Fingering her mass of curly, black hair, Sylvia's brown eyes go wide. "What?!!!"

Reaching for my water, I squeeze the freshly cut lemon into it, muttering, "Yep." As I take a sip, I spill the damn thing down my front, lemon bobbing onto the ground at our feet. "Shit!"

"Here!" Sylvia hands me her napkin, rising up to help.

"I'm fine."

"You don't look fine." She sits back down as I press the napkin into my wet blouse. "And don't think I didn't notice you guys were really stiff at the movies the other night, too."

"The break only lasted a night, Syl. We're back to normal I guess."

"What happened in Atlanta?"

What happened an hour north of Atlanta is what I really want to talk about, but I'm afraid she'll judge me for falling into Jaxson's arms so quickly after Ryan left.

"He didn't like my family. The feeling was mutual. I

brought up marriage."

"You didn't!"

"I did. And then he said he wanted a break. Even flew back early. Gave my parents this bullshit excuse. But by the time I returned home, which was the very next night by the way, he took it back." Bunching the damp napkin up I set it on the table and look around for a waiter, muttering, "Got me a bunch of flowers. Said he was sorry."

"Awwww," Sylvia smiles with a gushy, romantic look on her face. "What kind?"

"Doesn't matter." I grab her water since mine is gone and down a big gulp, so big I have to gasp for air after.

I'm really having a hard time with this conversation.

Jaxson hasn't called me.

And every day I stare at my phone wondering why not.

I've been trying to click back into Ryan but as the days pass that connection hasn't strengthened.

I feel like I'm a different woman now and the old me is a stranger. Like I'm walking in another person's shoes. Sleeping in bed with a man who is a stranger.

Something happened to me and I have no idea what to do about it.

"I know. It's so hot out," Sylvia says, explaining away my thirst. "I've been drinking like a dolphin."

Dying for a change in subject I ask, "How was the

retreat? I didn't get a chance to talk to you on our double date."

"I know, Rhett kept me all to himself. Isn't he beautiful?"

"His name is Harry."

"He looks like Rhett Butler, though. Don't you think?" Off my smile, she winks. "Belize was gorgeous! We had seven days of mediation, raw foods, probiotics, and yoga. If it weren't for the no-see-ems, it would have been perfect."

"What the hell is a no-see-em?"

She makes a face and leans in. "Little bugs so small you can't see 'em. *No see 'em.*" Off my laugh, she loudly complains, "Oh no, that's what they're called, and they're serious business! Invisible, flying creatures that bite you. Joy had a reaction to them. Remember her? Red welts all over her arms and legs. Her neck looked like she'd grown a goiter!" Through our laughter, Sylvia insists, "Oh, but the yoga, Rach! It was amazing. Just like Peru, remember that?"

"I'll never forget," I murmur as vivid memories play out the most relaxing week I've ever had. "They stopped yoga to enjoy the sunrise and sunset every day, then resumed class with us all in that state of awe."

"No phones allowed, except for pictures on the first day—"

"—Just to get it out of our systems!"

"Loved that," Sylvia smiles.

"But it wasn't raw-foods-only there. I don't think I would have enjoyed it as much if it were. Healthy eating I can do. Crazy eating? Um…no."

"You'd be surprised!" Off my cocked eyebrow, she confesses, "I brought snacks with me. I cheated."

Cheated.

There's that word.

Suddenly I need more water.

The waiter drops crackers with a bottle of garlic-infused olive oil at our table. Sylvia says, "Thank you."

As he goes to walk away I grab his arm. "Can you bring us more water?"

He nods and grabs my empty glass, heading off.

Sylvia is completely unaware of my inner turmoil. I'm lucky in her, to have a friend I feel safe with is priceless. But cheating is taboo. That's a stance I've always held. There is no grey area. Only black and white. And yet here I am in my one-day-break, having slept in another man's arms…and much, much more.

I want to tell her.

I need to tell her.

I'm fucking dying for help on this. But what if she judges me for it, or blows up like my mom did?

I can't lose Sylvia.

As she goes to grab a cracker I decide I have to keep this to myself. She glances to me and pauses. "You okay, Rachel?"

Before I know what I'm doing I blurt out, "I slept with someone the night we were on the break."

She throws the cracker back into the basket. "Holy shit! You what? Who??"

The story pours out of me. She soaks up every tiny detail, asking things like, "He punched Ryan?!" and "Ryan said he doesn't want kids?!" and "FOUR TIMES??!!"

"Five if you count the morning," I groan, laying my head in my hands.

"Holy shit, Rachel."

"I know." After I tell her what my mom advised about not divulging my transgressions to Ryan, I beg my best friend for the truth. "Should I tell him?"

"Hell no!" she mutters, leaning back to call the waiter. "Excuse me! We need some wine over here." She leans in to ask me, "Honey, how do you feel about this? How come you didn't call me the moment it happened? You must be killing yourself! He hasn't called at all?"

I'm staring at her. "You don't hate me?"

She blinks. "What?! No! I don't hate you! Now answer the question."

"What was the question?"

She leans in. "How the hell have you been surviving?"

"I've been trying keep my mind off it by writing about the trip for the blog –"

"What?!"

"—Not that part! About the farmers market, Atlanta, the restaurant we went to with my parents on Friday. Keeping the personal out of it."

Sylvia shakes her head and reaches over the table to touch my hand, her voice becoming very gentle. "Rachel, you can't leave out the personal in your editorials. That's what makes them so compelling! The drama, the nuances. That's what makes your writing great!"

"Thank you, but I think there's too much drama this time."

We order a couple glasses of Pinot Grigio from the overworked waiter at the same time a husky food runner sets our pastas down. Both men vanish while Sylvia and I stare at each other, dying for privacy.

"I never thought of myself as a cheater," I whisper.

She immediately counters, "No. Uh uh. He said he wanted a fucking break! No marriage. No kids. He flat out told you he didn't want what you did! And then he set you free and went crying back here." Off my resistant look, she leans in and firmly tells me, "You were a free woman. And not only free, but everything you thought was coming got stripped away from you. Of course you lost your shit!"

Tilting my head I mutter, "Come on. Isn't that a cop out?"

"Nope! Hell no!" Her head wags. "Honey, what were you supposed to do, beg him? You're not desperate, Rachel Sawyer, and Ryan should be kissing your ass right now. Especially in this city when there's too much competition and every man is looking for the next best thing, you have to listen when they tell you they're out! Or you'll find yourself cheated on."

"You make me feel so much better."

"Girl, the struggle is real." She goes to toast me, "You did what you had to do!"

But I hold my glass close to my chest, not willing to high-five with a drink. "If you love someone you don't go sleep with another man the first night you have a chance."

Sylvia drinks from her glass and thinks about this. "If that's how you feel — and I hear you — then why did you do it?"

Sighing, I confess, "Jaxson. He's always had this pull over me. I do what he wants me to."

Sylvia makes a noise. "No, honey. You do it because you *want* to."

I set my wine on the table to pick up my fork. My hand is shaking. She notices it. I whisper the thing that has been paining me the most. "It feels like I'm stuck in someone else's life."

"Look at your fucking hand, Rachel."

My phone rings and I literally jump in my seat, reaching to answer it, shoulders slumping when I see Ryan's name.

Staring at it, I set the cell on the table, unaware she was watching me.

Stabbing slippery penne with her fork, Sylvia mutters, "Mmhmm."

15

JAXSON

At the dimly lit, upscale restaurant Marcel, I'm hunched over the square-shaped bar listening to Jason and Justin argue about who gets the last french fry. Reaching into the metal basket I grab it and pop it into my mouth.

"Hey!" Jason shouts.

Justin laughs, "Now you know how it feels. Fucker."

That name was aimed at me.

I stare ahead.

"Okay," Justin begins. "You're normally not the most verbose man I've ever met, but tonight you're making mutes jealous of your prowess."

Shooting a half-smile his way, I mumble, "Prowess? Nice."

The bartender asks if we want another round. My twin

113

brothers start to turn him down but I usurp their haste with a firm and loud, "Yes."

"He has a voice when he wants to use it," Jason says, as he leans forward to see me better. His eyes catch something he wasn't expecting and under his breath he warns us, "Cora Williamson, twelve o'clock."

We face forward and act like we don't know she's gliding through the crowd toward us.

"Jaxson Cocker," her molasses voice calls out, "Never expected to see you in Atlanta on a Saturday night. No carrots to pull out of the weeds at this hour?"

Cocking an eyebrow to my right, I level her with a look that disintegrates her lofty air into ground-dust. Shifting her weight on five-inch heels, she adjusts the spaghetti strap on her black cocktail dress. It's perfect for this speak-easy vibe, and she wears it well. But then again looks were never her problem.

Justin quips, "Did you want something shoved up your —"

Jason hits him, cutting off the rest.

"Such a gentleman you are, Justin. Add some alcohol and that politician-charm just slips right back into the gutter it sprouted from, huh?"

Jason, who at first tried to protect her, cuts her down. "Did you see it down there when you were painting on that dress, Cora?" No one can talk that way to Justin and not have Jason cutting them to shreds. Except us other brothers, of course.

Her pretty brown eyes narrow and she slowly shakes her head like, *tsk tsk*, before focusing back on me. "You never called me."

"Nope," I exhale. "I didn't."

"Two months."

"I know how long we were together. Trying to forget it."

The bartender puts our drinks down and Cora uses that opportunity to lean on the bar. "Are you going to buy me a drink?"

I can feel the scoffs of my brothers beside me. And how they freeze when I tell the bartender, "Get her whatever she wants."

Victorious fire lights her eyes and she purrs, "Bombay Sapphire martini, please, Tom. Thank you."

"You got it, Cora." He leaves to grab the bottle from the glass shelves centered behind him.

I rise from my leather barstool and offer it to her, ignoring the subtle squirming of the twins to my left.

"Thank you," she smiles, eyeing me suspiciously. "Listen, about that land of yours."

Crossing my arms I cock an eyebrow at her. Who

knew the girliest girl at our elementary, middle and high school had a brain on her. She's grown into a commercial real estate broker and I don't like the way she's looking at me now, all business.

"What about it?"

"You're not using even half of it. Your cows only need a couple acres per beast for dairy production and your two horses are running free."

"My chickens like the space," I dryly tell her. "Hank's a desperado."

She tilts her head, smile betraying amusement. "Come on now."

"I'm not giving up my land."

"Selling is not giving up," she shoots back with a pretty smile.

It's occurred to me she'd be a welcome distraction to the obsessive almost dialing of Rachel's number I've been battling since she went back to New York three weeks ago.

Justin snorts to my left and I cut a quick glance to find him predictably wishing she would go away. "Jaxson loves every bit of that soil. You know he likes space. Remember?"

I smile at his protective dig. She does the opposite, giving him a look that would wilt a lesser man. He just grins at her, pearly whites glinting *I dare you to try a witty comeback. Bring it on.*

She drops it and returns to me, still all business, an attractive contrast in that sexy dress.

"Jaxson, I'm serious. I have a buyer who'd love to turn that beautiful land of yours into something even better."

Calmly I throw back, "Nothing's more beautiful than wide open pastures and oak trees older than America. Just because *you* were bored there doesn't mean anything."

She thanks Tom for the martini he's delicately placed on a white napkin before her. Taking a sip with all the grace of a lady, her eyes tell me she's not going to give up on the potential commission, but she would be willing to put it off for oh, say…a night.

Cora and I dated for a drop in time a year ago because she was familiar and I knew I wouldn't get attached. I like to be alone.

She can't boast that ability.

She wanted exclusivity immediately.

Not something I was ever going to give her. My body, sure, I'd give her that. Because it was in exchange for hers, and a man has needs.

She's not the type of woman a man like me can spend a lifetime with. For so many reasons I don't even have to list them to myself.

It was never even an option.

If she were more self-aware she'd have known never

to demand it. Not only was I not looking for a girlfriend, my lifestyle would never have made her happy anyway. Justin's lifestyle maybe. Or Jason's with all his parties and concerts and Hip-Hop celebrity friends. But she set her sights on me. That was her mistake.

The woman takes two hours to get ready for fuck's sake. What the hell?

But…like I said…I need the distraction tonight.

"Why don't you guys take off?" I tell the twins, entertained by how quickly their subtle shock shifts to amused acquiescence.

With a gleam in his pale green eyes, Jason jumps off his chair. "Well, we're gonna head out. I didn't want this drink anyway."

I stifle a grin.

Justin winks at her. "Interesting to see you again, Cora." He smacks my shoulder on his way out. "See you soon, yeah?"

"Yeah."

As soon as we're alone, Cora softens.

"How's Jeremy?"

"Good." I take Justin's abandoned seat, and languidly lift my scotch to my lips with my elbows on the bar. "His unit is in a peace zone right now. We Skyped two weeks ago. Mom tries twice a week."

She smiles sarcastically before licking a drip of condensation from her red-tipped finger. "I bet he loves that."

"You don't know anything about our family, Cora," I grumble, instantly protective.

"Touchy! What's wrong with you tonight?"

"Nothing."

"Yeah, that was convincing." She readies herself for another retort, but wisely decides it's not going to get her what she wants. "You look good," she says, instead.

I glance down to my black t-shirt and ripped blue jeans. The shirt is tighter than I like because the dryer did a number on it. "Nothing you haven't seen before."

Leaning in with sex all over her, Cora purrs, "Which is why I know how good you look, especially underneath all this unnecessary clothing."

I get a whiff of sweet perfume floating off her. It's subtle, but all it does is remind me of how good Rachel smelled in my soap.

It's as if she's right in front of me, her blue eyes sparkling up at me as her wavy hair splayed out on my pillow. What the fuck is going on with me?

Blinking away from Cora back to my Scotch, I mutter, "You still completely shaved?"

"I am."

"Drink up."

Taking one small sip she sets the mostly-full martini onto that napkin and watches me down my glass and slam it on the counter. Slipping her hand through my arm, I pay for the tab and lead her out of here.

There's a bridge from this to the structures that house the restaurants JCT Kitchen, Jeni's Ice Cream and also Bacchanalia. It's a romantic walk, the buildings darkly lit and well constructed ahead and the view of railroad tracks far below.

Because of this there are always a lot of pedestrians crossing it.

As we near the start I pull her away and back to where there's a dark, closed business with no one inside, and where people walking on the bridge can't see.

Cora's into it and soon we're making out like she didn't scream, "I never want to see you again, Jaxson Cocker!" the last date we had.

She's purring my name in between desperate kisses, and the desperation is all mine.

I groan into her neck, "Rachel…"

Cora goes stiff then pushes me off. "What did you just say?"

"Fuck," I grate, running my hands through my hair to smooth down the mess her clawing made.

She's so appalled her demand is hoarsely whispered, "Who the hell is Rachel?! Did you seriously just call me another woman's name?"

She has no idea Rachel is *the* Rachel, the one who was her close friend way back then. The one she accused me of liking when I ignored her in middle school. The one she always wanted to hate but couldn't because Rachel was so likable.

The Rachel I can't stop thinking about.

"I'm sorry. Your name is Cora. I know that. You know I do. I've known you for almost thirty years." Her eyes are as round as plums and her skin is starting to look that color. "Fuck. Look. This was a mistake."

I'm sure this has never happened to Cora. A lot of men would happily climb that tree, and they'd be thinking of no one else. Just of how lucky they were. Like how I felt when Rachel was in my arms.

Uncharacteristically vulnerable, she whispers, "Jaxson, what is happening?"

I clasp a firm hand on her shoulder. "I'm a dick, that's what's happening. I shouldn't have done this. I—"

"—You were using me to get over some woman named Rachel!"

"Fuck." I cross my arms, feeling terrible. "Okay, look Cora, I'm sorry. I really am. I'm in a bad place."

"You were always distant, Jaxson, but never cruel."

"Guess we're all capable of anything."

She stares, smoothing down her dress and holding her head high. "Yes, we are."

"Forgive me."

Her eyes have that dazed look people get after a car accident. She thinks about it, staring at me before she finally sighs, "I forgive you. But..." She smoothes down her hair, staring off before she locks eyes with me. "Don't use people, Jaxson. It's not okay."

My head bows as she walks past me, heels ticking along the concrete path to the bridge.

"Let me walk you to your car." I catch up with her, and we walk together like strangers.

My hands are in my pockets.

Hers clutch her purse.

When we finally get to her red Mercedes she turns to me.

"If you're so into this Rachel, why did you let her go?"

I don't have an answer for that, and she's shakes her head like she doesn't expect one.

She sighs, staring off at dozens of silent, parked cars. "Jaxson, you Cocker boys are such islands. Your family is incredibly insulated – no one can touch you. But you don't care because *you don't need anyone*. Isn't that what you told me?

'*I don't need anything or anyone outside of what I have?*' Well, it sounds like you might have found a woman who put a chink in your armor. Why don't you let her in it?"

She gracefully climbs into the sleek vehicle knowing I'm going to shut the door for her like I always did. Our eyes lock as she slides the key in the ignition. "Think on that offer I told you about. He's got serious money and it would take some of the burden off you."

"Cora, let me make something clear. That land is my soul. I'm not selling it."

I shut the door and watch her car's glowing red taillights drive away until they disappear.

Pulling out my phone I bring up Rachel's 212-number. My thumb hovers for several excruciating seconds.

I shove the damn thing back in my pocket and sit down right here in the parking lot with my head in my hands.

16

RACHEL

"Noooooo," I whisper as I stare at the slender plastic stick. Shuffling through the small paper bag, I pull out the backup pregnancy test I bought just in case this one was a lying sack of...

Three minutes later, there's another positive result.

Define 'positive.'

"This isn't happening," I breathe, rising from the side of our bathtub to stare at my reflection.

It was the nausea that made me wonder.

Three days of wishing I could replace my stomach with someone else's, every smell inspiring vomit – that's what had me worried.

But last night when Ryan made a move on me and had to jump back as I puked all over the duvet, I knew I had a big problem on my hands. And it wasn't the vodka from his law firm's party.

"Sylvia," I whisper into my cell phone.

"It's six o'clock! Why are you calling me?" she groans in her deepest voice.

"I'm pregnant."

I hear her jump up, pitch rising. "WHAT?!! Oh my God."

Feeling as though the bathroom is turning upside with me in it I whisper so he can't hear me, "Ryan said he's not ready to be a father."

"Rachel…is it even his?"

Tears start streaming.

It's been eight long weeks since I was in Jaxson's arms and not once has he called me.

With the dam breaking, I quietly whimper, "I was just starting to get my life back. I'm in the middle of a book on Peru. Ryan and I have been doing so well!"

"Have you? Because honey, when we all hung out Monday you didn't seem very happy."

"Oh God." I quietly put the toilet lid down so I can sit with my arms around my head, the cell clutched to my ear. "What am I gonna do?"

"Call Jaxson."

"No."

"Call him!"

"No. I can't. Even if it was his, if he doesn't want me then he certainly doesn't want this baby." We sit in silence. "I'll call you later."

"I'm here if you need me."

Facing my reflection I stare at the bags under my eyes. She's right. I'm not happy. I haven't been. I've been faking all of this. Writing has always been my joy, second only to reading, but writing about that retreat in Peru has been unnaturally hard considering how deeply I loved being there.

The sound of the coffee grinder sounds from the kitchen and I walk out to where Ryan's humming to himself in his sweats, no shirt, dark hair mussed up from sleeping soundly.

He glances over. "Hey beauty. Feeling better today?"

"I'm pregnant."

Ryan's hand freezes on the French press and he blinks away from me. "Oh."

Oh?

Jeez.

Who am I kidding? I feel the same.

Before our fight I'd been in denial about how little time we spent together, and how I wasn't truly happy. You can convince yourself of a lot when you're a creature of habit. We'd become one together, he and I, but I didn't know that until I stepped outside of our rut and did something crazy.

And Jaxson Cocker would of course be the instigator of 'crazy' for me.

Holding up the two sticks, Ryan stares at the impossible to ignore, pink plus-symbols. He nods and sucks on his lips, pouring the ground beans into the press and the boiling water over them.

"How did this happen, Rachel? I mean, I'm happy about it…but I thought we were using condoms for a reason."

Shit. I didn't even think about the fact that Jaxson and I didn't use any.

How did I let that slip my mind?

Because I was deliriously happy. That's why.

Oh my God. That means this baby is Jaxson's.

"They're not impervious," I whisper, feeling terrible.

Ryan nods. "True. And we did use those old ones when we ran out." Off my expression, he reminds me, "The ones from my old wallet? Remember when we went searching for it right before that trip to your parents?"

"The night of Avalon's party," I whisper.

My travel-book publishing house had a wild night where they rented out an empty loft space and featured for the fun of it a burlesque show, one that caused Ryan and I to get a little hungrier for each other than usual with all that fun sexual energy flying around.

Hell, we'd almost done it in the public bathroom at the event.

Trying to be a trooper, he forces a smile. "Well, if our child was conceived that night, it's going to be a handful."

The timing of this revelation is terrible.

It means this baby might be Ryan's.

What do I do if it is?

How do I even know if it is?

Tossing the sticks in the trash, I watch Ryan pull down two cups. He pauses and puts one away. His eyes are distant, thoughts miles into a future he said he doesn't want.

"What are you thinking? I know you said…" I can't even finish the damn sentence.

Ryan sighs and places both hands on the counter, the muscles in his arms tightening as he rests his weight on them and stares ahead. "Rachel, I wasn't ready to be a dad, but sometimes things happen." He locks eyes with me. "What do you want to do?"

"It might not be yours."

I did not plan to say that.

My lips part in surprise.

He blinks. "What?"

I have been holding that in for two months and now is when it slips out?

Unable to take it back and not even sure I want to, I whisper a shame-filled, "The night you left Atlanta…"

Before I can say more Ryan explodes. "You fucked *him*?!" Pacing around our small kitchen, he dents the fridge with his fist. "And here I thought they would have kept him in jail for the night." Flipping around, he shouts, "I even thought about that. *Hope they leave him in or maybe Rachel would have fucked him just to get back at me.* That actually went through my head!" Cutting a furious look to me he snarls, "I should have known. I should have fucking known. You've been different ever since!"

"And you've been the same."

"Because I've been trying to make a future for us!!"

"A future you said you didn't want."

"Don't pull that shit on me."

I'm too tired to pretend anymore. I just shrug, "You said it. You meant it. And your actions always showed it way before you had the courage to voice it to me. You weren't exactly happy when I said I was pregnant."

He jams a finger at me. "With someone else's baby!"

"I don't know that for sure," I mutter, knowing how lame it sounds.

"Fuck this shit!" He grabs his head and spins away from me toward the cabinets. "I can't believe this."

"I'm so sorry."

"Yeah. You're sorry," he groans. "Sure."

"Ryan, I'm not your first priority. I never have been. I just didn't know it until you told me."

He spins around. "If you want to get to the top you have to make sacrifices, Rachel. You knew when we started dating that I wanted to be partner and that means eighty, sometimes hundred-hour workweeks and being there whenever I'm needed. You were fine with it then. When did that change?!"

"I really need to wash my hands."

He motions to the sink.

I walk over feeling like a deer approaching an aimed rifle.

As the water runs over my soapy hands we are quiet.

He hands me a towel and I thank him, stepping backwards to put some distance between us.

"I'm just not happy, Ryan," I whisper.

His voice is barely contained. "Did *he* make you happy?"

Happier than I want to have felt.

But I won't rub that in Ryan's face especially since it doesn't mean anything now that Jaxson's never once reached out to me.

"It was an escape."

"Jesus," Ryan grates, walking past me. "That's just

great. You need a vacation from me? Take as long as you want!" I follow him into our bedroom where he pulls down my suitcase. "Here! Go!"

There is so much pain exploding between us. "Fine." I trudge to my dresser and yank open the top drawer, throwing panties and bras on our unmade bed.

"You don't know if the baby is mine," he groans. "I'm hurting here."

I stop and hold onto the dresser, tears slipping down my cheeks. There was a time when I loved him. When what he had to give was enough. But I know I was lying to myself back then. Over time Ryan Morrison's love for his job over family would have driven me fucking crazy and we would have gotten divorced.

And yet still, I do not want to hurt him. Especially when I'm hurting just as badly. There's a child coming. And we might be connected to each other for the rest of our lives.

"I'm so sorry, Ryan. I can't believe this happened to us."

"You should have thought of that before you let that fucking lowlife stick his cock in you!"

Like he lit a flaming match to dynamite, I blow up. "DON'T CALL HIM A LOWLIFE!"

"Oh fucking great. You're going to defend that piece of shit now? Huh? Oh, and I guess he wasn't your ex, either, huh? That bullshit about knowing him in grade school was a crock, wasn't it?!"

Tossing my clothes at the suitcase I growl, "I didn't lie about that to you. He was a childhood friend, maybe a crush, but I didn't lie to you."

"No, you just climbed into his bed the first second I wanted out."

I scream, "You wanted out!" Grabbing my stomach, I realize this baby doesn't need a screaming match in its DNA. "Ryan, we're done arguing. Go have your coffee and do what you love most. Work."

He glares at me then mutters, "Fucking slut," and storms out of the room.

I shut the door and start to sob.

17

JAXSON

The sound of a car driving up to my home in the quiet evening rouses me.

I set my book on the coffee table, and rise to see who it could be. Alberto wasn't scheduled to come by today at all and he never comes at night. Visitors are a rarity here.

Opening the door that faces west I step into a stunning pink and gold sunset as a yellow cab kicks a fog of dust into it, parking eight feet from my porch.

The back door opens and Rachel steps out, her beautiful blue eyes rising to meet mine.

I make quick strides down the three steps onto the gravel. "Rachel," I groan, so happy to see her.

"Jaxson," she whispers, with questions in her eyes. I don't know what she's doing here but by the rate my blood sped up to I can't wait to find out.

Pulling my wallet from my back jeans pocket I pay the man, glancing to the suitcase waiting on the torn backseat.

"Let me get that," I say from a distant place.

She steps back and shares a quiet look with me before I climb halfway in to grab it. Handing her the purse she'd left behind, I tell the driver, "Thank you. Have a good one."

"You too," he waves before trailing more dust in his wake.

Rachel walks slowly back with me to the house. "Is it okay if I stay with you a couple days?" she whispers like she's embarrassed to ask.

"Of course." I open the door for her to enter first. As she passes me I breathe her in, the scent I've missed so badly permeating my senses. Struck speechless, I set the suitcase under the iron coat hooks by my front door. The screen slams behind me and Rachel jumps.

I quickly mutter, "I still have to fix that," fixated on her.

"It's fine." White knuckles hold her purse as she slowly walks to the center of my living room, setting the small bag down by the book I was reading.

Pink and gold beams splash across her backside, turning her sandy-brown hair into ginger.

She's wearing a slender, silver anklet and I linger on it,

thinking of how many times I wanted to call her and didn't because I knew I had nothing to give her that could compare to her life.

And here she is looking like heaven in a form fitting, expensive dress that sure as shit doesn't belong on this ranch.

This beautiful woman's world isn't mine and everything about her is a reminder of that so I keep my mouth shut and wait for her to explain her sudden appearance.

Fuck I want to touch her.

Hold her.

And all I can do is shove my hands in my pockets and wait.

My gaze travels to the novel as she says, "Tuesdays with Morrie. I loved that book."

"Might need some tissues before it's done."

"As if Jaxson Cocker would ever cry over a novel," she smiles.

"True," I smirk and it makes her smile fade.

She holds my look, both of us with a hundred unspoken questions and wants.

Tears start to gather in her bright blue eyes.

In a voice harsher than I mean to use, I ask, "Another fight with your boyfriend?"

She closes her eyes a moment, turning away from me.

The answer is obviously yes.

So I'm her man-on-the-side.

I can't be that.

Not a day has gone by that something hasn't happened to remind me of her smile, her laugh, her naked body welcoming me in.

I had to switch soaps because it drove me nuts to smell the stuff.

How does one night stick with a man like that?

It ain't right. And it sure as hell ain't fun.

I don't want to go through withdrawals all over again, and yet here I am saying she can stay.

I am going to regret this, aren't I?

Her eyelashes drift up and she looks at me over her gentle shoulder, appearing more like the little girl I once knew than a New York socialite. As a tear slips down her cheek she confesses, "I'm so sorry. I don't know what I'm doing. I'm lost Jaxson. I haven't been right since I was here."

Blinking in confusion, I confess, "Neither have I."

She stares at me a moment and then whispers, "Oh God. I'm so afraid of what you're going to say when I tell you this."

Cocking my head, I ask,

"Tell me what?"

Wringing her hands, she shakes her head and stares at

the floor.

"I'm pregnant, Jaxson. And I don't know if it's yours or Ryan's."

The air leaves the room.

I don't blink.

I don't move.

She gazes at me, blue eyes filling up. There's a quicker rise and fall of her lungs now.

She's not only scared, she's terrified.

Realizing I had this all wrong I clear my throat, my voice hoarse as I rasp, "You need a place to think then." Blinking hard I go back for her suitcase, my stride slow and steady. "They can test for that."

"I don't know. Can they?"

"Yeah," I mutter with my thoughts on an unknown future, one in which this child might be mine. The other where I have to send her back to Ryan for the last time if it's his.

With my eyes cast to the floor, I realize I can't let that happen. "I don't know the details but we'll be able to know who the father is before it's even born." I meet her eyes.

"Oh. Well, that's something I guess," she mutters, hugging herself.

I nod, feeling like a sledgehammer has crashed into my psyche.

And here I thought she was coming for an affair.

"Stay as long as you need. I'll sleep on the couch, so you can clear your head." I stop with my boot on the first stair. "Rachel, no matter what happens, I'm your friend. And I'll always be here if you need me."

Her lips part and I head upstairs.

I feel oddly calm as I set her suitcases on a table for her ease, making sure the zipper is facing in the right direction. I change the sheets so she has a comfortable place to rest.

One thing keeps rising to the top of my spinning thoughts – she came to me.

Downstairs I find her still hugging herself but now in front of one of my long windows, the clouds grey now that the sun has completed its descent.

Her shaking breath hitches as I walk up to her, wrapping my arms around her from behind. After a pause, she leans into me and closes her eyes. "I'm in over my head."

"Shhhhh. It's okay. There's no rushing anything, not on my land. It's against my religion. Are you tired?"

"So tired," she whispers.

"Why don't you go lie down and get some rest?"

She touches my hands and I release her, watching her head for my bedroom.

There's a baby growing inside of her, and it might be

mine.

A Cocker boy or girl who might look at me and call me daddy.

Jesus.

A deep frown cuts into my brow as I watch Rachel slip out of her heels and leave them behind the couch. It's where we found them in the morning when she was here last, but I don't think she's aware of that right now. She looks out of it.

As she touches the staircase railing I call over, low and steady, "I'm glad you're here."

She turns her head and holds my calm gaze, her spine melting a little as she sees I mean it. Another tear slips down on her sad smile, "Thank you. This means so much, you don't even know."

"Well, I tormented you enough when we were kids. Figure I owe you a bit of rest."

On a small laugh, she pads upstairs like there are weights on her legs.

It's only seven thirty now, but I don't expect her to come back down tonight.

Leaning against a wood beam, I gaze out at my ranch seeking answers only nature's beauty can provide.

18

RACHEL

I slept really well last night, surprisingly. It's so quiet here. No sirens or honking or construction. And Jaxson was so kind considering what I'm going through – what we're going through – that it set my mind at ease just enough to allow exhaustion to pull me into sleep as soon my head hit the pillow. When you don't feel like you're under attack, it's easier to exist.

What will this baby be like, I wonder as I touch my bare abdomen.

Will you be a boy or a girl?

Don't worry. I don't have a preference.

I'm just asking.

I've always wanted children, and while I didn't want them this way I feel it's time to get stronger and face the music, but strength feels impossible to reach.

I don't want him or her to feel unwanted.

"Would be nice to know who your father is, though" I whisper, touching my stomach as I move my abandoned dress so I can rifle through the suitcase Jaxson was considerate enough to lay on a table.

A small whisper inches into my mind. The chances of those condoms being old enough to not work aren't high. It's much more probable that the man who slept on the couch last night, the boy I climbed trees with, is this child's father. Standing up I run a hand through my hair because the idea of that feels a little too good.

But that doesn't mean Jaxson feels the same. How could he? He never once reached out to me. And here I am thrusting myself into his life with a dilemma a weaker man would run from.

I won't ask him for anything. I just need to rest and get my head and heart in a better place.

Tugging on white jeans that soon won't fit me, and a pale blue cotton t-shirt I wear around the apartment back home, and my running shoes, I tiptoe downstairs to get some water.

Jaxson's throw blanket is strewn over an empty couch, and the guest bathroom door is open. The kitchen is also silent and empty.

I look for him on the porch and exhale as I spot his Jeep still parked where it was when I arrived.

That means he didn't run screaming into the night, thank God.

Loud mooing in the barn pulls me there. I find Jaxson detaching some kind of contraption from the cow's udders. He's in a cowboy hat, faded jeans, work boots, shirtless, with latex gloves protecting him – or maybe the cows? – from germs.

Hearing me, he glances over his wide, naked back and holds my eyes a beat, then goes back to what can't be paused, his tattoos and muscles rippling with every move he makes.

I feel like I'm taking advantage of him by showing up here and start to turn away.

The cow objects and he soothes her, "Hey, Con, easy girl. She's got nothing on you."

Laughing under my breath, I stop and say, "Thanks a lot."

He flashes me a handsome grin, but remains focused. "Grab that bucket for me?"

Suddenly I'm helping, following his instructions and trying to keep up. One after the other we bring the milk to a tank, and detach udders from a vacuum-milking machine. One thing I can say about it, you're not thinking of anything else when you're doing this. I completely forget for a while the drama I'm in, and soon I'm smiling.

"What's this one's name?" I ask, pointing to a sweet-eyed, spotted cow. "She seems to like me."

"That's Flo. She does like you. But then again, she likes everyone."

"No, I think it's just me."

Jaxson grins, so good-looking it's almost too much. "Nah, she likes everybody because she's a slut," he jokes.

My smile vanishes so quickly that Jaxson rises up from his stool. To avoid him I drag the final bucket to the cooling tank and pour the fresh milk in.

Frowning, Jaxson opens the gate and touches each cow as she passes him on her way out onto the open range. "Alright, ladies, eat all the grass you want out there. No one's selling any of it today."

That caught my attention, but I'm too shy around him right now to ask what he meant by it.

Strolling over, he checks the cooling tank to make sure it's shut tight, pushing a couple buttons before pulling off his gloves.

I follow his lead and pull mine off, too, also tossing them in a can marked for recycling.

As I turn to face him, my breath hitches.

Jaxson's casual and friendly manner is gone and his dark green eyes are intently set on me with a look that is at once fierce and protective. "Your boyfriend called you a slut when you told him, didn't he?"

I can't look away. "Yes."

Jaxson's nostrils flare like a bull's. "Fucking asshole!"

"He was really angry, Jaxson."

"And he had a right to be. But he never should've called you that!"

My voice is gentle as I ask, "Shouldn't he?"

A crease slices into Jaxson's forehead and he leans in to tell me, "No. He shouldn't. It's not what you say to someone you love."

Filled with guilt I argue, "I don't know about that. People say things all the time they don't mean."

Jaxson's calm demeanor returns and he nods once like he's figured something out. He heads for the door and mutters, "You still love him."

"Jaxson…"

"You came here to rest." That his voice is more distant does not go unnoticed by me as he adds, "I won't bring it up again." As I follow him silently outside his volume shifts like he doesn't want to upset me anymore. "Ever have eggs fresh off a farm, not from a store?" I shake my head. "Let's go say hello to more of my girls."

He leads the way to a beautifully constructed chicken coop off about ten yards, but again, I'm bad with distance. Its east wall is golden under the rising sun, the fiery outline making the large structure even more impressive. "Did you build that?"

"I did."

"All on your own?"

He laughs. "Yes." When he turns and walks backward after his horses nay in the distance, Jaxson cocks his cowboy hat back on his head to see them better, and as I drink in the golden outline on his body I catch sight of the tat that doesn't really match the one that runs the length of his arm.

I'd seen it the last time I was here and had traced the letter and thorns, but I hadn't asked about it. Now, so I can keep the air light, I point and ask, "What's the C for?"

He smiles and flips around, walking like only a man can. "Stands for Cocker. My brothers and I all have this tattoo, some on our chests, others, our arms."

"When did you get them?"

"When we were eighteen. Actually I was twenty, Jett was eighteen, when he and I designed them. The younger brothers had to wait until they hit legal age, when Dad couldn't bitch." He smirks over his naked shoulder at me as he reaches for the latch to the coop. "But I think he wants the tat for himself. He feels left out. We all think that."

"I can't imagine a congressman with a tattoo."

His eyebrows go up. "So you know my dad's a

congressman?"

"My mom told me. She secretly hates it."

"Why would she hate it?"

"I have no idea."

He laughs in his subtle way and grabs a carton for today's eggs. "Hello Gertrude. Now now now, calm down." Feathers have gone everywhere. I start laughing as two other hens join her to fly around his head and make him duck with his calloused hands up for cover.

He loves this farm, that's plain as the feather that just landed on my shoulder. He comes alive here, green eyes sparkling like crazy. I can't help but feel lighter the more we keep away from the subject of me and Ryan...and me and him.

"You miss Hank? Is that what you're tellin' me?" he laughs as the hens fly.

"Is Hank the rooster I heard this morning?"

As the birds calm down, Jaxson fills up the carton with eggs from large nests. "You heard Hank? You didn't last time."

I yelp as a hen comes running at me. "Yikes! Let me outta here."

"They're not used to a woman being with me. They're jealous. Just like Connie was."

The stunning glint of mischief in his eyes makes me

slow to reply.

I want my child to have that.

Glancing away I mumble, "The rooster was here last time?"

"He's been with me two years. You didn't hear him because you were…kinda wiped out." Jaxson winks, dips out of the coop, and holds the door for me. "Hurry before they get out. Oh shit. Hold these." I take the carton from him as he chases a stray chicken around, catching it by the legs and murmuring to it as he puts it back inside.

We walk back to the house in silence and he opens and holds the door for me there, too, his arm up high so I can walk under. "You always do that."

"What? Open the door?"

"Yeah."

"Doesn't every man?"

On a sarcastic smile, I whisper, "Nope."

Jaxson takes his cowboy hat off and sets it down. His sandy-brown hair, the same color as mine, is mussed up. He doesn't go to fix it. He just gazes at me with intense concentration. Then he takes my chin in hand. "You should have every door opened for you."

With uncertainty growing inside my womb, this sweetness makes me want to cry. On a sharp intake of breath, I force the tears back. "You're being very good to me."

He leans in and kisses my nose then touches his forehead to mine like he wishes he could kiss me in a less friendly manner. "You should wash the latex off your hands before we have breakfast." How the hell did he make that sound sexy? "I'm going upstairs to change. Tilly got my jeans all muddy." As he heads off, he adds, "And I can see you staring at my chest, so I'll put a shirt on so as not to distract you."

Gaping at him, I cry out, "Cocky jerk!"

Jaxson grins. "Tell me you haven't been staring at this." Both his index fingers point at his chest.

"Nope. Not interested in the slightest."

"Yeah, right," he scoffs. At the bottom of the stairs he stops, jaw ticking as he stares at the floor. "I don't know what I want, Rachel."

With my heart twisting up, I tell my best childhood friend a lie. "Me neither."

Slow and steady, he walks out of my sight.

19

JAXSON

"No, you sit. You're my guest," I motion to one of the tall stools next to my kitchen island. The stove is embedded in it so she can stay nearby while I cook, right where I want her to be. I believe it's my job to put her at ease.

She came here for rest.

I can give her that.

And I want her to feel safe with me.

Morning sun streaks in through the windows as I grab bacon, butter, Himalayan salt and a homemade, unsliced loaf of bread.

"What're those green things?" Rachel asks when I set it down by her hand.

"Rosemary. She makes this with virgin olive oil. Fucking delicious."

"Who does?"

Pulling out a cast-iron skillet, I turn up the gas stove and start separating the bacon to ready it. "Patty and Lou live up the street. He grows grains. She bakes bread."

"Perfect combination," Rachel smiles.

"They've been together thirty-one years last month. Never seen 'em fight. But then again, I don't live with 'em." A smirk flashes on my face and I glance to find Rachel staring at me like I'm a ghost.

I know the feeling.

Having her here without the sex clouding everything is feeling a little too good.

Like she's always been here. Like my loner days are over and somehow I don't mind.

Ignoring this feeling, I explain, "I buy as much from the locals as I can. We support each other. With Patty and Lou we just exchange bread for eggs and milk. Which they use to make more bread. Keeps going on like that."

Rachel lazily watches me cracking eggs into a bowl to add a little milk and cream cheese to. She leans on her elbow and wistfully says, "In New York I don't even know who lives right next door to me in the same apartment building."

I mutter, "Sounds lonely."

"You never know who they could be. A lot of crazies," she explains.

On a shrug I disagree, "I tend to trust people until they show me otherwise. People usually rise to the occasion when you treat them like they will. If they don't, I deal with them then."

She watches as I lay the bacon side by side in the skillet, crackling oil shooting up. "Tell me what happened after I moved away from Atlanta."

While the eggs wait until the last second to be cooked, I grab a serrated knife to slice the fresh bread and tell her the story of my childhood. I'm not a talkative man usually, my brothers would tell anyone that.

I don't think Rachel would agree. We used to talk all the time about Dickens, Shakespeare and Tolkien, the books most kids our age thought were too 'hard' to read.

It doesn't feel like a chore as I tell her, "Jett and I caused a lot of hell all the way until after we graduated. Oh, you probably remember him as Jerald. He's Jett now. The two of us paved the way for Justin and Jason to have caution-tape strapped to their heads before they even made it to high school. Remember them?" I glance to her and raise my eyebrows. She nods. "Well, Justin became Class President despite the faculty campaigning to have him taken off the ballots after he'd slept with one of the teachers." Seeing her reaction, I grin. "Don't worry. It wasn't the teacher's fault. He went after her without mercy. Poor girl was interning from college and she was a beauty. He was almost eighteen. She was twenty. Justin's defense was, if she's going to teach looking like that she'd better resort to first grade where the boys wouldn't notice. The school kept it under wraps only to save our reputation."

"You mean their reputation?"

"No. Ours. My dad's position has power."

"Oh," she whispers, shaking her head. "Wow."

I hand her a medium-sized piece of bread to taste and she takes a bite. "Good huh?"

"That's amazing," she gushes, popping the rest in her mouth. "Name one of the things you and Jerald – sorry, Jett – did that was so awful."

With a spark in my eyes I don't miss a beat. "We turned on the sprinklers at five of the dances. With enough time between – years sometimes – that no one ever saw it coming."

"You didn't!"

Chuckling, I nod, deciding to keep the less attractive and funny adventures to myself. "Oh yeah! We sure did. All those dresses soaked to their bodies? Good stuff."

Rachel laughs, "What about—"

Reading her mind, I finish her sentence, "—Jason? Well, when they were kids it was mostly Justin who was the bad influence and Jason followed. When he grew up, that fucking guy developed a bad habit of falling in love with the wrong woman. Someone stuck too big a heart in him. We have to bail him out of bat-shit crazy situations too often. The most recent was a model with a coke addiction."

"Oh no," Rachel murmurs, watching me work. "I lost a couple of good friends to cocaine in my early twenties."

"Yeah. We almost lost Jason but it turns out he's addicted to women, not drugs." Remembering the Bernie-drama, I shake my head and mutter, "Which are sometimes more dangerous than drugs. Hand me that spatula? Thanks. Do you remember Jake?" Rachel stretches and shakes her head. My eyes flicker to her belly and I focus back on scrambling the eggs. "You were probably too young to remember since he was only four or something. Were you ever in our house, other than when your parents came for dinner?"

"One of the nights you threw pebbles on my window you brought me back to your home when everyone was sleeping," Rachel smiles.

"Oh yeah!" A smile flashes over me at the memory of us tiptoeing upstairs. I pretended I was gonna knock on each door I went by which made Rachel cringe every time. Meeting her eyes for a moment, the years disappear. "I should have kissed you then."

"Why didn't you?"

"We were eight."

"Nine was better?"

Hot oil spatters from the bacon skillet onto my arm and I turn the burner off, locking eyes with her right afterward. "I think our first kiss was perfect…and worth the wait." Rachel slowly nods her agreement. I go to touch her hand and pull back before contact, shaking my head and switching off the egg's burner next. "Jett and I were both in basketball and football in school." Glancing to see if she's impressed, I'm satisfied she is, so I continue, "Jett went into boxing. He went semi-pro but gave it up when he found The Ciphers."

"So he's in a gang."

"A motorcycle club. But I guess they do tear it up pretty good." Quietly chuckling to myself over some of the shit my brother has pulled with The Ciphers I spin around to get plates. When I turn back I catch her checking out my ass, and hold her look to let her know I saw. On a deep smirk, I tell her, "I put on a shirt to make it easy for you, Rach, but I can't help how well these jeans fit me."

Shaking her head she smiles. "Lord, you've got an ego on you."

"I just don't want to confuse you with these." Flexing my pecs under the cotton, I stretch my wide chest out more so she can enjoy the show. She starts laughing and my smirk shifts to a genuine smile.

That's all I wanted - to relax her shoulders some more and wipe that frown from her eyes. Behind her smiles I keep seeing pain. I can't take it.

The plates get piled high. I even add wild blackberries as I go on, "I was offered a scholarship to play college and I went, but I was far more interested in organic farming and horticulture as a whole. The lifestyle suited me more than parties and concussions."

"Less women throwing themselves at you, too," Rachel says, with a hint of curiosity.

Pouring coffee, I don't answer that. Hell, I'm considering whether or not I want to. But I'm not the type who hides shit or defends my actions, so when I bring the cups to the island I lock eyes with her and wait a beat.

"I've had more than my share, Rachel. I'm no angel but I've tried to do right by them." Cora's face flashes to my mind. The look in her eyes when I called her Rachel. I was using her. "Most times, anyway," I mutter. "Grab these?"

She nods and takes the cups while I carry everything else out to my porch. There's a nice, dark walnut table there I found at an antique store.

New, forest green patio furniture is on the other side of the front door.

On days when it's not too hot, I like to be outside as

much as possible, listening to the cicadas and watching my animals graze.

"I didn't realize how hungry I was," Rachel whispers, after we've eaten in silence a while.

"When did you eat last?"

"Don't remember," she admits, long eyelashes rising slowly to take in the view. "It's so beautiful here, Jaxson. I feel almost calm now."

"You look more relaxed. Still a little nervous, though."

She laughs and makes a face. "You're too honest."

"No such thing as too honest."

"Mmm," she whispers, glancing back to her food.

"You haven't touched your coffee."

She looks at me with meaning.

"Oh, shit," I mutter. "Sorry. I'm an idiot."

"It's okay. I like to smell it."

The sound of a vehicle approaching catches my ear. While I shovel eggs onto Patty's bread, I watch the place where the car will soon come into view. Seconds later an S.U.V. kicks dust up as it parks.

My blood starts pumping.

Her boyfriend may have found her.

"This him?"

Rachel's staring, too. "No," she quietly says.

As the dust settles, we can see behind the windshield

and an older man gets out and hobbles over with a cane like he just walked off the pages of an Ernest Hemingway novel.

I walk out to greet him, brushing my hands on my jeans.

"Jaxson Cocker?" he asks in a thick and slow Georgian accent.

"Yes, sir."

"Cora Williamson told me you're looking to sell some of this beautiful land." He sweeps his cane through the air behind him.

My blood grows edges as I narrow my eyes, hooking my thumbs in my belt loops. "She told you wrong. I made it clear I'm not selling."

"Oh now, don't get your hackles raised," he chuckles. "I don't want all of it. Just about a hundred acres or so. I can pay good money, son!"

"What's your name?"

"Leroy Jarvis at your service."

My eyebrows rise, but I shake his outstretched hand, the cane falling from where he'd perched it on his leg. I get to it first.

"Oh, thank you. Darndest thing. Can't avoid it, though."

Not that I have any intention of selling my property, but he's an interesting character and I'm curious. "What do you want my land for?"

"Well my wife has it in her head that a women's center would be beneficial to the community."

I was expecting the words 'condominium' or 'shopping mall.' My tension ebbs away. "Well, Mr. Jarvis, I appreciate the idea."

He cocks an eye at me, leaning forward. "So you're not opposed to it?"

"I'm not for it, either. There aren't enough people up here to warrant that, for one thing. And I like things the way they are. But I'm glad to have met you. It'll have to happen someplace else."

Sensing my finality, he glances to Rachel who's walked up to stand in the porch's doorframe behind me. I look over my shoulder, hold her gaze a moment and realize off her look that she heard Cora's name.

"I understand. Let me give you my card," the old man says. "We don't have any children, you see, me and Liana. Now that we're retired, there isn't much to do. She's not the type to sit on her behind all day long. Not my Liana." He winks and hands me a business card, throwing a smiling, polite nod to Rachel. As he hobbles away, he calls out, "It would mean the world to us!"

She and I watch until he's out of sight, then I cast my eyes down and wait for it.

Don't have to wait long.

"Cora Williamson? Now, that's a surprise."

Squinting away the sun, I hold Rachel's beautiful blue eyes. "I'm not going to deny it."

"When did that start? When I left?"

Can't help but snort, "Yeah. Right after. That's me. Ten year old playboy."

Rachel smiles, but her eyes are betraying how she really feels about me with one of her childhood friends.

"When then?"

"About a year ago when she finally broke me down. Lasted a long time."

"How long?"

"Two months. Not exclusive. Serious stuff."

An amused grin slowly spreads on her soft pink lips, clearing away the cloud of discomfort and jealousy. Can't say I'm not pleased she cares, though.

Staring off at my land, Rachel says, "Two months. Wow. Guess you bought a ring and everything."

"Yep. A cock ring."

"Jaxson!" she cries out, laughing through it.

Chuckling, I walk back to her thinking how much I want to touch her, but that's not a good idea since she just got here and there are too many questions that need answering before sex fogs our minds again.

From those three steps taller, she loses the smile as we gaze at each other, now almost the same height. I get mesmerized by how the sun is lighting up her skin, her bright blue eyes slightly hooded as the chemistry crackles between our bodies. Before I know what I'm doing, I confess, "Rachel, I've never asked anyone to marry me, but you."

Her eyelashes float closed and she takes a long, quiet breath.

This is the moment I could take her hand and pull her down into my embrace.

But I don't.

It doesn't feel right to do anything other than be her friend until we have answers, until I know I won't get my dick kicked in again when she leaves.

She might be having another man's baby.

If it's his, I won't fault her for wanting to see if they can work things out.

The child deserves it.

But fuck if I'm not beginning to pray it's mine.

20

RACHEL

Coming out of the bathroom from yet another losing of my meal, I wipe tears from my eyes and glance over to find Jaxson lying on the couch with a fresh hardback perched on his knee, the other leg over the side, his bare foot resting on the throw rug.

I've been here five days and he's been wonderful. He jokes when I get too serious, and says nothing when I need to think.

We've made meals together and told some of our stories, keeping away from the subject of Ryan.

He knows all about Sylvia now, and how it took me some time to find a good girlfriend I really connected with after I finished college at NYU, when so many of my friends moved back to the states they were raised in.

He confided to me that Jett is still his best friend, even though he's rarely in Georgia anymore. How Jett stayed with him for Jake's wedding and they stayed up late drinking beers, cooking dinners, and just being men together. "I love all my brothers though, as if they were my kids more than my equals. Dad says I was born a man."

I smiled and said I would have to agree. "Maybe that's why you rebelled against the teachers. You didn't like being treated like a child."

He smiled at that.

And then there's the farm labor. Helping him collect eggs to sell to the local grocer as well as milking the cows every morning, has had a very soothing effect on my nerves.

The vomiting fights to remind me what's really happening, though, and then my world comes crashing in again as reality hits.

The silences with Jaxson are not edgy like they often are with Ryan. Jaxson rarely knows where his phone is much less being always on it, and hardly anyone calls.

Ryan is always checking his cell, obsessed with winning and staying ahead.

Ahead of what, exactly?

With Jaxson, there is no competition, like the world is spinning outside and he's simply observing, disinterested in engaging in their game.

It bores him, and the farm thrills him.

* * *

Petting his horses Harry and Hermione in the grey light of dusk two nights ago I asked, "Why didn't you name them Harry and Ginny?"

As he stroked the stallion's muscular neck and I pet the mare's, Jaxson explained, "Harry Potter should have ended up with Hermione, not Ron. Hermione was a muggle. Harry was raised by them and could understand her better. Ron was a good enough guy, but he's not Harry. Isn't that right, Harry?" The horse glanced back to Jaxson. "See? He agrees."

I laughed, "He recognized his name, that's all." I went back to petting Hermione, finding comfort in how she bent her neck to add pressure to the caresses. She loved being petted.

Jaxson said, "Nah, it's more than that," his smile drifting away as he laced thick fingers into the stallion's mane. "Are you bored, Rachel?"

Taken slightly aback, I whispered, "No. Not bored at all." I locked eyes with him and reached to adjust his cowboy hat. "There. Now I can see your face better."

"Maybe I want to be mysterious," he smirked, looking so damn handsome.

On a small smile I confessed, "Jaxson, you don't need a hat for that. You were born mysterious."

He searched me. "No, just quiet is all. Simple man. What you see is what you get." The thoughtfulness in his tone implied he wondered if I liked that about him. I couldn't express how much, and so I just explained why I believed what I said.

"I've come to you for something and you've given it to me without even asking what it is."

"What's to ask? I already knew what you needed."

As my heart pounded, I stammered, "Why come here? That would be one question."

Without warning, he pulled me to him as his green eyes held mine with unwavering steadiness. His voice was thick with needing me to understand him. "Rachel, this is my home because of the peace it gives me. When you stayed over that first night, you had a glimpse of it. I know you came here for that, but I also know you came to see if there was anything between us that could last."

I held my breath, quieted by the truth of this.

He released me with a look that said if he didn't, he'd carry me upstairs. "Are you hungry?"

I nodded and watched him head for the house, following with goosebumps down my arms.

* * *

All day yesterday he kept his distance. Today has been the same.

He hears me return and glances over his shoulder. "Ginger ale didn't help?" he asks, deep and calm.

"I'm afraid not," I murmur and walk to the window to

watch Harry and Hermione grazing in the waning light of evening. Minutes lazily pass until the horses decide to move on. I watch them gracefully vanish from my line of vision before I ask him, "What are you reading?"

"Power of Now."

"Hard not to think about the future."

"Always is."

"Especially under these circumstances."

I hear the book close and turn to watch him rise and come to me. I'm silenced by the look in his eyes, the platonic friend is gone. He's advancing on me like he did that first time I was here. I've been waiting for that look, and dreading it, too.

What if this baby is Ryan's? What will I do?

Everything I've built is in New York City.

So why am I feeling like I never want to leave this ranch?

I know the reason. It's staring at me from behind emerald green eyes I want to stay lost in.

But am I just seeking solace?

Is this just an escape?

"Rachel…" He leans down, surprising me by brushing his lips ever so softly against mine. It feels so good I want him to do it again. "I've gotta make that frown go away for good."

With my lips tingling, I shake my head. "You've been perfect, Jaxson. There's nothing more you can do."

He asks, "Nothing?"

"Oh my God," I whisper as he pulls me to him.

21

RACHEL

"It's been so hard not to touch you."

"For me too," I breathe, loving the strength of his arms around me again.

I've been feeling so weak.

I need this.

I need him to carry me. I'm filled with shame over that, but God help me, I need his strength now. Being here with Jaxson makes everything seem like it's going to be all right no matter what happens. I wish I had that feeling in myself but I just don't.

And to hear he wants me as much as I want him, that these last, chaste days haven't been easy for him either is the kind of validation I need to hear. I've been longing for his touch.

Like he's speaking from within my own heart he confesses "It's been fucking torture for me being this close to you and not touching you."

Riddled with insecurity, I murmur, "You haven't shown it…"

He takes my chin in hand like he likes to do. I have to admit I love being held here. His forcing me to look at him means I don't have to find a reason to look away.

Jaxson crushes me in one of those hot kisses that have haunted me ever since I tasted them. I melt into his body and respond with equal abandon as he tightens his arms around me. Tracing his lips down my neck he thickly says, "Let me inside."

My voice is no more than a whisper. "I'm scared of how I feel about you."

"I know. This is the first time in my life that I've felt this out of control," he groans, lifting me up and devouring me with kisses that don't stop all the way up the stairs.

Setting me down in his bedroom with such care as though I might break, Jaxson begins to undress me until I'm completely bared to him. As each strip of clothing falls away his breathing grows shorter with need, but his fingers never rush.

He strips his t-shirt off from the back forward, mussing his hair. I lay my hands on his naked chest as he slides his jeans' zipper down and kicks them off. "You're so beautiful."

"Some might say I'm glowing," I mutter, attempting a joke and knowing the timing is awful.

His green eyes narrow, but he shakes his head and takes my chin again. "Some would *swear* it."

I moan as he pulls our naked bodies together, his erection pressed against me. The closeness this shared time has given us has only heightened my desire for him.

I'm aching for everything he is.

Jaxson makes love to me in a whole new way than that first night when everything felt naughty, a little dirty and almost wrong.

Everything tonight builds slowly.

His hands run the course of my body like he's got nowhere else to be for about fifty years.

His grip is strong, protective and like I belong to him.

His kisses are deep, molding my lips as though he's claiming me.

We move together like we were made to be here and I feel emotions welling in my chest.

The kisses are languid yet passionate, like molasses coming to a slow boil.

When the pleasure builds to its height in both of our bodies, his thickened cock continues to fills me with slow moving, sure strokes until I am arching my breasts into his chest and whimpering his name.

We climax together, moaning and biting each other's lips.

When he pulls back and I see there are tears in Jaxson's eyes, mine go liquid, too.

Afterward we remain entwined and confused and at peace.

He buries his face in my hair. Throbbing inside me in the aftermath. Gripping me to him.

It's the most emotional sex I've ever known and as he gazes at me, I know it's the same for him.

Crushed in a delirious vice of muscles and tangled emotion, I silently send a prayer up to God if he's listening, *Please, if you're up there, please let Jaxson be my child's father.*

I know what I've been fighting so hard to deny ever since he teased my nine-year-old self, *"That's because you're in love with me!"*

Even though I threw every objection I could think of at him, *"As if! You only wish! Ha! Keep dreaming!"*

…He was right.

I am deeply in love with him.

22

JAXSON

This was the first morning I didn't hear Hank's crow in the years I've had him.

From a deep dream where Rachel and I are alone on a beach with soothing, pale blue waves, a knock on the front door rouses me at the late hour of nine o'clock.

She murmurs, "Did you hear that," peaceful blue eyes cracking open.

We were sleeping in each other's arms, faces so close you'd think we wouldn't be able to breathe enough oxygen. Yet I was comfortable.

I rise onto my elbows and listen. "Yeah. I wasn't sure if I did, but since you—" Another, louder knock interrupts me. Throwing off the blankets I pull on my jeans. "Stay here."

"Oh my God," she whispers, sitting up with a start.

"What if it's him?"

"Just wait here," I order her again as another knock sounds. No one shows up here without giving word or receiving invitation.

I know it's not that Mr. Jarvis – he's too polite a personality to pull something like waking a man on a Sunday in his own home.

Sniffing the air for a potential brush fire I exhale, satisfied my land is safe.

Reason implies it can only be one person. And his timing is for shit. I stroll down the stairs readying myself for a battle. If this guy thinks he's going to take her from me today he's fucking wrong.

Swinging open the door, I blink at a face I haven't seen in two decades, but who looks so alike the one I just left it's jarring. "Mrs. Sawyer…"

"Is my daughter here?" Ellen Sawyer demands, rising on her toes to look past me.

The sound of quick padding down the staircase turns me around. Rachel is smoothing her hair, back in the clothes I peeled from her body last night. "Mom!"

I step back to allow our unhappy guest entry, and receive a scathing look from blue eyes very much like her daughter's, only older. "I hoped he was wrong."

"Mom, what are you doing here?" Rachel whispers.

"What are *you* doing here!!??" Pale hands fly up and cover Ellen's face as she careens away like we're poisonous.

Her eyes make a quick inspection of my clean kitchen.

Pacing briskly to do the same of the living room side of my home's open floor plan, she shoots me a look, one that prepares me for another outburst, probably worse than the last.

I have no idea why she's looking at my home like it's a piece of shit. No money was spared here. The windows are double paned. The furniture was personally designed for me to my specifications, save for a few pieces I found in antique stores. Even the fucking pots hanging over my stove are the best available. The Cocker family comes from old money. I'm no slouch. And while I live rurally I enjoy quality as much as the next man. Any woman with her upbringing would be able to see the value of my house and everything in it.

It's me she disapproves of.

And only me.

To her everything here is just a symbol of me.

"Can I talk to my daughter alone, please?"

Rachel crosses to stand at my side. I glance down to find her calm and in control of herself. She takes my hand and squeezes it. Ellen's blue eyes drop and widen as if Rachel touched a scorpion. What the fuck is this woman's problem?

"I'm not a child, Mom. I don't need to be chastised or

scolded. Jaxson has been very good to me. And this is his home so I won't ask him to leave so you can—"

But she doesn't get a chance to finish. "—You're pregnant! That's what he told me. Is it true?"

Rachel's mouth parts in surprise. "*Ryan* told you?"

"He told me, yes, he told me! And when I demanded to know why he didn't know where you were, and why was he calling *me*, he coldly informed me you don't know who the father is!!! And that I might look for you 'at that loser's house.'"

I grip Rachel's hand harder as she begins to melt.
"Mom…"

"You told me you didn't sleep with him!" She points at me, eyes wild with fury. "You lied to me!"

Rachel's eyelashes flutter to me.

My eyes tell her I don't fucking care if she had to lie about that first night to protect herself from this she-bitch. Like I give a shit what she told her mother. This woman isn't important to me. Her daughter is, and only her.

Rachel blinks away from me to say, "I'm sorry, Mom, but you were so upset, I didn't feel I could confide in you."

Huffing, Ellen rakes her hands through her dyed-brown hair. As her arms fly up pieces stick out all over her head. "This can't be happening. It's payment for what I've done. I thought I paid enough!" Mumbling almost inaudibly and rubbing her face, she repeats, "I thought I paid."

Rachel tugs her hand from mine and goes to console her. "Mother, stop it. Why are you this upset? Is this because of…?" She quiets, not wanting to say something aloud in front of me.

Now I'm curious. What has made this woman so upset with me?

Ellen fearfully whispers, "Because of what, Rachel?"

"Mom you don't even like Ryan, but you're acting like I cheated on my husband of twenty years! And that morning I came back to your house it seemed like maybe you were acting out of your own guilt there, too. You were taking it so *personally*." Her voice grows more gentle as she asks, "Mom, did you cheat on Dad? Or is this over Tanya and…oh, I don't know! I just can't understand why you're this upset."

"Oh Rachel," Ellen whispers, face crumbling.

"You don't have to tell me, but Jaxson and I are not the same thing. Ryan and I were unhappy for a long time. We're not married. He doesn't want to be married."

Ellen's eyes are stricken. Nothing Rachel's said has abated her concern.

Does she really hate me this much?

Choked with emotion, she rocks the room to dust. "My affair was with Michael Cocker, Rachel."

Icy nails slice into my spine. My dad?

No.

No way.

No fucking way in hell did Dad cheat on my mom.

Ellen's eyes lock on me, his eldest son. "Michael Cocker and I were in love. For *years*."

"No," I growl, stepping forward. "He never cheated on my mother. No!"

But even as I say it the conversation with my mom replays in my mind with a whole new understanding.

"They lived two doors down from us when I was in grade school. You had them over for dinner sometimes."

"You mean John and Ellen? ...Ellen and I were acquaintances. She fought me at every turn at the Atlanta Woman's Club."

Fighting it, I growl. "It's not possible."

"It's the reason we moved away," Mrs. Sawyer moans. "I told John, and we wanted to try and make it work. I couldn't do that with Michael two doors away."

"...but then their family moved to New York out of the blue. John got a job or something..."

"None of you were ever meant to know."

With tight fists I cross to the window, seeing my father in bed with this woman. I can barely speak, but I have to. "Does my mother know?"

"I don't think so."

177

Turning on her, I shout, "Why the fuck are you telling me this now?!"

She collapses to the floor, weeping. I go to help her up and Rachel rushes to do the same. Her body is trembling as she stares up at the two of us, looming above her. "You don't understand," she whispers. "He might be your father, Rachel."

I let go of her arm and back away.

Rachel rises slowly.

She turns and stares at me.

"No," I groan. "No!"

How similar we are. How well we get along. Our love of books and silence. Our fucking hair color.

The magnet that's always pulled us together.

"Oh no, Jaxson," Rachel whispers. "What have we done? What if…"

I croak, "Holy shit. The baby…if it's mine."

Rachel starts to sob, "Oh my God! Jaxson, we…"

I rush to pull her in my arms. "We didn't know! We didn't know."

I can feel Ellen's stare. I jam a finger at her. "You! TALK."

Ellen struggles to stand. "I need a cigarette." She goes for her bag fumbling with the zipper as I stroke Rachel's hair, her body shaking with sobs.

Flashes of us that first night are tearing up my insides. It's fucking brutal how graphic they play out and how tainted they become in seconds. And then last night.

"Go get some air," I tell Rachel. "I need coffee. It's too early for this shit."

Rachel nods and follows her mother to the porch, both of them wilted.

I whisper under my breath now that I'm alone, "What the fuck am I gonna do?"

My first thought is to call Jett, my best friend, but this will kill him, too.

I need to take this hit on my own until I have more information.

I need to listen to Ellen's story first.

Find out what the fuck went down, if she's just lost her marbles or if Rachel really could be my half-sister.

I need details before any of this can be processed.

But holy fuck. I feel like I'm gonna puke.

Gripping the kitchen counter with both hands, I stare out at my horses grazing in the distance. When I introduced Rachel to them and explained why I didn't name the female Ginny, I was thinking of Rachel, telling her in my subtle way how I felt about her. That she was who I belonged with. That I knew it when I was just a kid, when no one thinks you know anything – I knew she was for me.

When she moved away I made myself forget.

Was it just because we're family that we were drawn to be together? Did we just misunderstand the soul connection?

"Shit!" I slam my hands on the counter and hold back tears.

Until last night I wasn't sure I could raise this baby as my own child even if it wasn't mine. But that shifted. When Rachel and I made love something happened to me.

I was ready to step up, even if it was Ryan's. I knew nobody would ever take her away from me again like her parents did when they moved away.

And now...

"Fuck!" Yanking the brewed coffee pot out so fast, some splashes out. I pour until the cup overflows, and swear again. Exhaling disgust at this whole situation, I make quick strides to join them and find out how the fuck this happened.

23

RACHEL

My hand is cradling my abdomen as I stare off.

I can't breathe.

I can't think.

Jaxson...

And a man who was not my father might have raised me.

All these years might have been a lie. All the Christmases. All the birthdays. Going with my parents to the Cocker house for dinner and that man might have been my real father.

My mom is smoking her second cigarette, lit up as soon as the other went to the nub. She quit years ago. Must have picked up the pack on the way here.

I can't imagine what she must have been feeling when

she heard from Ryan who I was with, and how long I'd been in Georgia.

She and I haven't said a word after she whispered, "Rachel," and I croaked, "Shut up."

I woke up with our limbs entwined, blissfully enmeshed and knowing I love him. And now he might be my brother.

Jaxson explodes onto the porch, coffee splashing unnoticed as he locks eyes with me. He's tortured, too. We're both having a hard time looking at each other, so much pain.

Numbness starts to take hold of me as I watch him plant his feet and bark at my mother, "When did it start?"

Mom's staring off into his ranch. The cows are making a lot of noise in the barn. No one was there to let them out. I heard them in our silence while we waited, but Jaxson hasn't noticed.

He wants answers. So do I.

As memories play out before her distant blue eyes, Mom tells the story she's held from us for decades. "You never plan these things you see. John and I moved a couple houses down from the Cockers during a difficult time. We were having trouble conceiving. It was putting a strain on our marriage. I'd had three miscarriages, and wanted a baby more than anything." She takes a slow drag on the cigarette. "Michael was so handsome. So charming. So easy to talk to you just as neighbors. We didn't plan the affair. No one ever does, I think. But I ran into him quite by chance when I was visiting my mother in D.C. Michael was there working for a congressman, hoping to be one himself someday. We had lunch and then..." She inhales sharply at the memory's strength. "I lied to my mother and said I had to go home early. Instead I went to Michael's hotel. He didn't want to let me in anymore than I wanted to be there. But the chemistry was too strong for us, and he'd given me the key already. It was too hard for me to turn it down. And with me standing there, he let me in." She closes her eyes and whispers, "Shortly after, I became pregnant. But so did Nancy. Michael said my baby might not be his. I hated him for that, but agreed to keep quiet, even to keep it from John. We tried to stop, but time and again we weren't able to resist the pull. It was too strong and we weren't."

Jaxson growls, "Mr. Sawyer found out."

My mom glances to him from her daze and whispers, "Yes. Eventually he did. And he made me choose. We had to move. The first year in New York was one of the hardest of my life. The withdrawals from Michael were so painful."

"Mom," I groan, covering my face. "How could you guys keep this from us?"

She shrugs, defeated. "When you were kids, it didn't matter. You were too little for me to worry that something

183

would happen between you. But then when you ran off with him I saw his Jeep and knew who it was, first I shouted, then I called and called. I was going to tell you then but—"

"—I left my phone there."

"Imagine my horror when I heard it in the guest room," she takes a drag off the cigarette, the damage done. "I didn't know where he lived or I would have driven here. And I didn't have the courage to ask Nancy then. Michael and I have never spoken since I moved away."

Jaxson asks, "You talked to my mom today?" He's glaring at her like he might rip her throat out.

"Jaxson, calm down," I whisper.

"Calm down? Do you know what she did to us?!"

"It wasn't just me!" Mom cries out. "No one ever blames the man!"

This truism sinks into Jaxson instantly and with fists clenched he spins around to punch a hole in one of his screen windows. "Did you tell my mom about this?" he growls, protective of Nancy Cocker, the woman I remember my mother disliking. Now I know why.

"No! Of course not. I told her there was an emergency. She doesn't know anything. She didn't even know Rachel was here. I didn't tell her about the baby." Mom covers her face with the cigarette poking out. "My God, the baby."

I croak in pain, "Oh Mom!"

"I'm so sorry Rachel honey. I should have told you a long time ago. This is all my fault."

"And my father's," Jaxson growls, pacing to gulp his coffee and slam the cup back on the table. "Why did you come back to Atlanta, Ellen? To see him? Because I won't let that happen."

She scoffs, "I most certainly did not come back for Michael. Forty years with a good man makes you love him more than you did when you were young and foolish. I don't want to be with your father, Jaxson! I don't care if I ever see him again. But my John was raised here. This is his home and he wants to die here. I promised him he has nothing to fear, and he doesn't. Not from me."

Bile rises to be dealt with. I rush inside and release more vomit than I think I ate food. Washing my face off with the coldest water from Jaxson's well, I stare at my reflection and realize I have to make a choice.

Returning to the patio, I find my mother alone. "Where is he?"

"Milking the fucking cows," she mutters, pulling a long drag from a fresh cigarette.

In bare feet I rush out to the barn. Jaxson's faced away from me, applying the milking machine to Connie's udders as she tells him exactly how she feels about him being late. Poor thing is in pain.

His back tenses as he hears me come in.

"We're going to get tested, Jaxson. DNA. That's what we have to do."

He looks over his hunched shoulder. "Who can we trust?"

"I don't know. I don't live here."

He stares at me and a dawning anger darkens his face. "I know who."

24

JAXSON

Doctor Lee Saurnet has excused himself to close the blinds of his private practice. Today his waiting room feels claustrophobically small. The receptionist is absent for secrecy — yet another way of making this feel all the more disgusting.

Ellen and John Sawyer sit on a single chair with her in it, looking like she needs another cigarette. He's balanced on the arm, holding her hand, silently staring forward, his decision to face this head on resolute. But then again, he's had years to digest this bullshit.

Rachel is chewing her fingernails on the farthest chair from her parents, and won't look at either of them. Occasionally she glances to me and I catch it every time, like

I know she's about to. We're in sync, and it's driving us both crazy. I growl, "This is fucking ridiculous," and walk to put my hand on her shoulder for support.

Her eyelashes rise slowly as she lifts her head to me. She closes her eyes and touches my hand, holding it so I won't leave.

I catch her mom watching us and shoot at her, "What? I'm not abandoning her during this just because you fucked up. If they find out we're…" I can't even say the word siblings. "…it's not going to change the fact that I'm her friend."

A knock sounds on the door, so familiar it can be only one person. My father.

I swing it open with judgment and condemnation all over me.

"Jaxson," he says, his voice solemn. Stepping inside, he glances behind him. "Did anyone see you come here?"

"You mean Mom? No, she wasn't strolling down this street by happy coincidence, Dad. What took *you* so fuckin' long?"

At my cussing, he frowns, but doesn't have the balls to call me on it like he did with Jett when they fought at Jake's wedding. This time our perfect congressman father is the one in the doghouse.

But I'm not relishing it.

It's a sad day in a man's life when his father falls off the pedestal.

He enters, locks the door and sees the Sawyers. They remain seated, both of them holding his look.

"John. Ellen. I know I said it back then, but…I'm very sorry about this."

Mr. Sawyer's cleanly shaven jaw clenches as he inhales through his nose. I can tell by his face he's imagining his wife and my father in bed. Even today you can see the appeal of my dad, his presence powerful, his height formidable, and his looks haven't dipped in age. John Sawyer is by all appearances average, but a good man. Can't say my father is that right now.

Ellen's blue eyes cast downward, her grip tightening on her husband's hand.

My dad glances to me as he turns to address Rachel. "I'm very sorry we've put you in this position." She nods, teary eyed as she stares at who might be her biological father. Tense and curt, he politely continues, "We hoped it would never—"

"Cut the crap, Dad!" I shout. "You should have forced your hand! You might be her father! Do you understand what that means?"

His pale green eyes cut to me, and steel. "Of course I do, Jaxson." Glancing to my fists, his voice softens. "I need you to understand if we had told your mother, you boys would have been raised in a broken home and turned out very differently than you have." He struggles against unexpected emotion, and confesses, "Jerald might never have been born. Or Justin, Jason..." he stops, unable to continue.

He loves us.

I know that.

But now I've learned something else by this confession.

He loved Ellen, too.

So much that he thought of leaving Mom after Ellen got pregnant with Rachel and when I was on the way, too.

I stare at him in shock, then rub my face like I want it clean of this mess. Whispering to myself, "That's why it went on for years." He couldn't stop seeing her because he loved her. I blink into a past where my brothers were never born.

Dad scans everyone's faces, guilty of being honest and of saying something that hurts everyone in this room. He returns to me with imploring eyes as he calmly says in his stoic way, "I love your mom. You know I do. I never meant to hurt her, or John. This was nothing we wanted and we fought it. Things aren't always black and white."

Rachel gets up, pulling my focus.

"I have to throw up again," she whispers. Her eyes dart to her mother before she vanishes down the hall. The

190

doctor passes her and asks if she's all right. "No."

Wearing golfing pants and a Polo shirt, Dr. Saurnet shakes hands with his college friend, his expression somber as he tries to cover his personal reaction at how far this affair has spun out of control. "Michael."

"Lee. Thank you for leaving your golf game to help us."

He shakes his head. "I owe you for '97. Don't give it another thought. So, it's going to be a simple blood test since you're all here."

Ellen asks, "What about a prenatal test for the baby?"

"How far is your daughter along?"

Ellen looks to me for the answer, realizing suddenly that she has no idea.

"Nine weeks," I tell him, crossing my arms and feeling heavy.

Dr. Saurnet nods, pursing his lips a moment. "It's safer to do after she's twelve weeks but we can do a test now where we inject a needle into the womb —"

"—You're not poking needles in her."

My father looks at me. "Jaxson."

"No! First find out if Rachel is my sister. Then we wait until the child is *safe* before we go digging around, potentially hurting it."

Like my brothers and I do when we don't like

something, Dad shoves his hands in his pockets, his lips a thin line.

I cut my focus back to the doctor. "So Doc, let's start pulling blood samples. Dad, you first."

My father has always been my hero. Today he's just a man. Human. Flawed. And I hate him for that. Every motherfucking second of this bullshit is tearing me apart.

We are all quiet as one after the other Dad, John and then Rachel, walk back to get their blood drawn. Rachel is so pale she's scaring me.

As we wait for her, the deciding factor in how deep this debacle goes, I cut a look to my dad as he rolls down his sleeve, warily watching me.

"If she's your daughter you are a piece of shit."

"Jaxson, you need to cool down."

"Cool down?!" I get in his face. "She might be my sister! And do you know what we've been doing?! Do you!?" Agony rips into me and I punch my own chest. "You could never know how this feels! If you had been honest, she and I never would have happened!"

I shove him and storm out of the office into the sunlight of a bright Sunday afternoon. Birds are fucking chirping. Stupid cars are driving by with their windows down, music from their radios blurring past me.

The world is still spinning, but to me it's ended.

For the first time in my life, I'm not proud to be Michael Cocker's son.

25

RACHEL

"Did I hear Jaxson leave?" I ask the room. Mr. Cocker locks eyes with me and exhales through his nose like Jaxson does when he's containing his emotions. He nods once.

I look over at the father who raised me, and who I love dearly. He's looking at me like he might lose me. I walk over to whisper, "Dad?" He rises up to take my outstretched hands. "Whatever happens with those tests, you are my real father."

Tears jump to his eyes. He pulls me into a hug and says into my hair, "My sweet girl. I'm so sorry. I should have told you but from the second you were born I loved you. When I found out, I didn't want to share you. It was selfish. I'm so sorry."

He sobs into my shoulder and I just want to escape. "I

194

have to go," I tell him, pulling away and heading for the door.

Mom calls after me, her voice cracking, "Rachel!"

I ignore her.

As the sunlight hits me something else does, too.

I'm a hypocrite.

I'm pregnant. And I don't know whose it is.

She was here years ago in these same shoes, only there were marriage vows involved.

But right now Jaxson's hurting, too, and probably almost as much as I am because both of us know we may have committed a mortal sin. I need to be with him.

We promised we would be friends.

And we will be.

Even if that's all we'll ever be again.

I love him and I will watch him get married to someone else and carry it to my grave that I loved him once, more than I should have.

Searching the sidewalk in both directions, I feel peculiar and separate from my body, like this is not my skin. My hand travels to my stomach and I wince as stubborn nausea continues to claws at me.

"Rachel, I'm here." Jaxson Cocker steps out from a shadowed divot in the building next door. "What now?"

We walk to meet each other.

In a hushed voice, I explain, "He said normally he'd

send tests back to the lab."

Jaxson exhales through his nose, eyes on the ground.

"But since my dad called in a favor and we're a scandal, he's running them himself."

"He'll have the results tonight, Jaxson. In a few hours. He'll call you directly as you asked him to."

"I need some time to get ready for this anyway."

"Me too." I step closer to make him look at me. "Can we go to the ranch? I want to be where it's quiet."

Rubbing his face like he's trying to scrub reality from his skin, Jaxson says, "Come on."

Hearing those two words cuts me to my core.

He almost takes my hand and then decides against it, swearing under his breath. He walks around the Jeep and opens the passenger door for me, but doesn't touch me.

"Friends can still help someone into a car," I gently tell him.

"Rachel, I can't." His teeth are gritted together as I climb in and he shuts the door hard.

26

RACHEL

Jaxson's ranch normally has the soothing effect of a massage followed by a long hot bath plus two days of sleep, but with all that's happened we are having a hard time allowing that tranquility in.

He made lunch.

We barely touched it.

My mother has left messages I can't listen to.

Jaxson's phone has rung, too.

He ignored it when he saw it was his father. The doctor promised to call Jaxson directly, so he knew Michael wasn't calling with results. Just more problems.

I'm on the front porch now, staring off and numb with worry.

Suddenly the screen door slams. I glance over to see

Jaxson with his cowboy hat on, arms crossed like he's made a decision. "I know what we can do to relax."

"What?"

"We're going to ride my horses."

I face the calming view again, my voice distant as I turn him down. "I've never ridden a horse before. I'd be too scared."

"Yep. So scared you'll forget about the phone call."

"Oh, so you know I'll be scared?" I glance over and see a smirk on his face.

"I have no doubt," he chuckles.

"You think that little of me?" I toss back, growing slightly irritated.

"I think you're a scaredy cat, Rachel Sawyer."

I blink at him and then surprisingly laugh for the first time today. "How many times have you called me that?!"

Like a kid, he says, "A million. No, a trillion times... plus one, now." As I smile at him trying to cheer us up, he jerks his chin to the door. "Come on."

After Jaxson saddles Hermione up for me in the corral he tugs on the front and flank cinches to make sure they're secure.

"They don't have riders often, so be prepared for anything."

I just shake my head because I know he's goading me.

His appearance of severity vanishes in a grin. "Hook your foot in here." He holds the chestnut brown leather stirrup and helps me slide my sneaker into it. "Now throw your leg over and hold onto the horn. There. That's good."

From atop the seat I gasp, "She's taller than I expected."

Jaxson chuckles, "How's the world look from up there?"

"Gorgeous," I smile, meeting his eyes.

His smile flickers and he nods, turning to give the cinches on Harry's saddle a tug before petting the enormous beast. He mounts him and grabs the reins, looking incredibly handsome.

Desperate to stop thinking of him in that way, I lean down and pet my horse, closing my eyes and readying myself for my first horse ride.

Jaxson says, "I hate to tell you this but Hermione's the alpha so you're gonna be leading. I hope you know how to control her."

My head whips to him. "What?!"

He laughs and languidly tells me in his deep voice, "I'm kidding. She always follows Harry's lead. All you have to do is hold the reins gently in hand and let her do the rest."

Mashing my lips together I grumble, "You're not nice, Jaxson."

"Who said I was?" he smirks, giving Harry's reins a tug. The stallion breaks into a calm strut and Hermione gently follows, clip clopping out of the corral into the late afternoon.

The breathtaking view of lime green grass, oak trees, and cows grazing under fluffy white and grey clouds go unseen, because I'm fucking terrified.

"How you doin'?" Jaxson glances over his shoulder, green eyes sparkling with amusement.

"Great. Just great," I lie.

We head out into the pasture at a slow pace. The strength of the horse underneath me is unnerving, because I can feel how truly powerful she is. I know I'm not in control. If she broke into a gallop I would have no idea what to do. But she stays calm and serene, following Harry.

Soon I'm loosening up and enjoying myself. After a while of gentle riding I begin to feel we are one. My body is rocking with hers in perfect balance as if I was made for this. I pet her neck, bending over to whisper in her soft ear, "Thank you for going easy on me."

A few feet ahead of us, Harry's long tail glides back and forth as Jaxson calls from him, "What'd you say to her?"

Drinking in the sprawling, sun-kissed view for what feels like the first time I call back, "Just something between us girls."

Jaxson makes a face like that answer isn't good enough. To get back at me, he says to Harry, "Hey boy, should we go faster?"

"Don't you dare!"

He winks over his shoulder and jerks the reins. Harry breaks into a swift trot.

Sure enough, Hermione follows her boyfriend's lead. As she speeds up I begin to bounce, and my legs tighten against her sides.

Jaxson pulls his horse's reins sharply right and turns Harry around to trot beside my horse and me.

I stare at him, eyes wide. "Aren't you supposed to be up there so she knows what to do?"

"How ya doin' Rach?"

"Answer my question!"

"Wanna go faster?"

"Hell no!"

He grins and gives Harry's side a light kick, egging the horse to again take the lead but this time at a gallop. Hermione doesn't listen to me as I urgently tell her, "You don't have to do everything he says!"

I might as well be talking to myself.

"Make your grip firm. Trust the horse!" Jaxson calls back. We gallop to the farthest point, the wind whipping through my hair and goosebumps all over me. A grin travels up from my soul.

At the farthest point Jaxson guides Harry to turn around and Hermione obeys the move with graceful ease, slowing the gallop to a nice, steady clip as we head in the other direction.

"You're a natural," Jaxson smiles, no longer teasing me.

Feeling lighter than I have in months, I laugh under my breath and close my eyes a second. "That was very exciting! Can we go faster again?"

"We sure can!"

For over an hour the horses disintegrate our troubles. The bright sun warms our skin and eases our tormented souls. Freedom of spirit replaces worry. And somehow Hermione's strength starts to become my own.

As we ride closer to the house, Jaxson frowns and cranes his head. "You hear that?"

Inside, both our phones are simultaneously ringing, overlapping each other.

"Whoa, boy," he tells the stallion bringing him to a stop. Jumping off first, Jaxson rushes to help me down.

As he goes to release my hand, I grip his to keep him here a moment longer.

"Jaxson," I whisper, holding his worried eyes. "Whatever happens, please be my friend."

On a sharp intake of breath, he pulls me in for a quick hug. "Always."

He holds the door for me and we go to our phones, exchanging a look as we dial.

"Mom?"

My mother's voice is trembling. "Rachel. I'm so sorry."

"Oh God." I whisper, eyes locked on Jaxson's hunched back.

She breaks down crying, choking out, "John is your father, Rachel. It's John."

Jaxson turns and meets my eyes, the phone clutched in his right hand. He's listening to the same news from the doctor. "Thank you, Dr. Saurnet," he rasps, emotions barely controlled as he hangs up, eyes locked on mine.

27

JAXSON

"Shit," I groan, tossing the phone on the couch and my hat with it. Running my hands through my hair, I grip my head a second longer and sit down on one of my leather chairs.

Rachel walks to lean against one of the wood beams. She hugs herself, her blue eyes floating around the room as reality sets in that I'm not her half-brother. We didn't commit one of the worst sins known to man.

The nauseating idea of what we'd done and how we feel about each other despite it is lifting slowly off both of us.

"Wow," Rachel whispers.

In times like this I stay put until I know what to do. So right now I don't move. Not for a long time. A sharp intake of breath from Rachel makes me look at her.

She's staring at me. For how long I don't know. "I think I need to see my father, Jaxson. I think he needs me. I need him, too."

"I understand. Are you coming back?"

She blinks to the floor and shakes her head. "I have to go home, I think. I'm on a deadline with my editor and I haven't written a single word here." Off my silence she quietly add, "And I still feel too weird."

"I know. Me too."

The urge to offer her a place to write as long as she wants, right there on my dining table – hell, I'll even buy her a desk – gets shoved down. She's right. We can't exactly just start right back up where we left off. I'm having a hard time looking at her. I'm so angry with my father. This day has been a rollercoaster of pain.

And besides, her reminding me of her deadline also reminds me of who she is. What do I have to offer a city girl like Rachel?

"I understand." Running my hands through my hair in my struggle against all of this, I ask, "What about the baby?"

"Oh God, the baby," she whispers, closing her eyes in relief that the child is not born of accidental incest. But it still might be Ryan's. Blinking rapidly while she thinks of what to do, she finally says, "He told me about the paternity tests. It's safer to wait until after twelve weeks. Ten is good, he said, but twelve is better. I want to make sure it's safe. Especially after the grief of today. So much stress on it. It has to feel what I've been feeling."

I wag my head like someone's punched me. "That's three weeks." *Three weeks without knowing. Three weeks without seeing you.* "You want to do that in New York?"

She licks her lips and looks out the window. "I need to get my life in order."

And your life is there.

"I get it," I rasp, staring off.

"Jaxson," she whispers, walking to sit on the couch and lay her hand on my knee. "What do you want?"

"I want you to be happy."

She holds my eyes a moment then withdraws her hand, leaving an emptiness behind. "Will you drive me back to Atlanta?"

Now?

Jesus.

My phone rings and we both glance to find the word 'Dad' on the screen.

"Are you going to answer it?" she asks.

"No."

On a deep breath, Rachel reaches to the phone and hits, 'decline,' sending him to voicemail. She opens her palm

206

and I slide mine onto it, gripping her fingers. "Jaxson, thank you for letting me come here and clear my head."

On a sarcastic smirk, I mutter, "Yeah. Real relaxing."

She squeezes my fingers "Don't be like that. It was. Riding Hermione today made me feel like myself again. Even with that horrible test result looming over us, she gave me the strength to face what I have to now. And Jaxson, even with us not being brother and sister, I still learned my parents kept something from me that could have changed everything. I need to go home after I see my dad, get my life figured out." Putting her head in her hands, she sighs, "I have a lot of feelings that need to be sorted through." Meeting my eyes again she softly says, "I don't know what the next step is, but there's a bridge that has to be crossed, and a decision to be made."

Jealousy lashes into my veins – a feeling I never felt before I met her.

She's talking about Ryan.

I felt this when I saw him kiss her.

I felt it when I didn't talk to her for two months.

And here it fucking is again.

Releasing her hand I rise up and go for my keys.

"I have to pack." Rachel reminds me, heading for the stairs with heavy steps.

Exhaling, I watch her climb them, then walk to my

kitchen where the horses are grazing outside the window with their saddles still on. Heading out to take care of that, I call up, "I'll be outside."

The ride to Atlanta for the second time today is unnerving for a different reason than this morning.

She's leaving.

I've been given the right to love her.

But now…she's leaving.

As we pull up to Arden Road I grip the steering wheel and shove down the desire to ask her to stay. I don't feel I have anything to offer her here. To ask her to milk cows for a living, and spend lazy days with me, doesn't seem right or remotely plausible.

I carry her suitcase to the house and Rachel remains by my side, quiet and frowning as deeply as I am. The door swings open and her mother is there with bloodshot eyes and a cigarette in her hand.

"Jaxson," Ellen whispers. "Come in."

My throat is dry as I shake my head. "I'm just dropping Rachel off."

Her surprise is an exhausted flicker across her face. She blinks between Rachel and I on the porch and then drops her gaze. "I'll give you a moment." She lifts the suitcase and when the front door closes, I turn to the woman I made a promise to.

"Rachel, if you need anything remember I'm your friend. If you want me to come up for the paternity test, I will fly to New York without hesitation."

She touches my cheek, her angelic blue eyes filling up. "Can I let you know?"

"Sure," I whisper, pressing her hand into my stubbled skin. I pull her into me and squeeze her tightly, whispering into her soft, hair. "I want to be there. This isn't just lip service. I'm a man of my word."

She nods and pulls away.

Struggling, I mutter, "It might be mine. Promise me you'll tell me either way."

Her eyes go wide. "Of course!"

My throat is closing. "We'll always be friends."

"Always," she whispers with a look I can't decipher because I'm too fucked up inside. But over the coming weeks I'll replay it over and over.

She goes into the house, pausing to hold my eyes before she closes the door.

My heart collapses. I raise my fist to knock hard, but stop just short. Cocker men don't beg. Shoving shaking hands in my pockets I walk to my Jeep and don't look back.

28

JAXSON

My mom looks as fresh as a pink rose as she answers the door minutes later. "Well, what's the occasion?!" she smiles, her pretty brown eyes glittering with surprise. "Come in! You want some lemonade?"

"I'd love some, Mom," I say with a forced smile.

She happily heads for the kitchen while telling me about her day.

"You just missed Jake and his new wife! I wish I knew you were coming. I would have asked them to stay longer. We had a delicious lunch and then I kept them late showing her pictures of Jake all the way from when he was a baby on up! He hated it," Mom laughs. "You would have enjoyed watching him squirm."

As I follow her into the kitchen, I glance up the stairs

to see if Dad is here.

He's who I came for.

But now I just might have to tell her the truth on my own.

As she pours the lemonade she goes on, "Remember that photo of Jake on the donkey? That man who went door-to-door for kid's pictures? And Jake was too big for the thing but I wanted the photograph so I forced him? Remember that?"

I nod. "I wasn't home that day. Thank God."

"But you remember the photo?"

"How could I forget? Jake looked like he wanted to kill the photographer."

Mom laughs, "He did!" Looking wistful, she pours tall glasses for both of us. "Oh, I want a granddaughter, Jaxson. I so hope they have one. All these boys! Never one daughter to cuddle with and dress up. You guys couldn't care less about shopping. When Jett's girlfriend came here it was such a relief to have someone who needed my help! Anyway, I told Jake to get on it."

She hands me her homemade lemonade and I stare at it thinking of all the BBQs she made this for. This and her famous fresh ginger ale that Jason always hoards. All those good times when we didn't know Dad was in love with another women, too.

My younger brothers' faces flash before me.

"Is Dad home?" I ask, readying myself to break the news.

"No, he isn't. Earlier today an emergency came up and he looked like someone died or something. He hasn't been back since." As she goes on about how irritating it is to be married to a politician because of the confidentiality of the matters he deals with daily, I watch her face.

She's in love with him.

Has been, my whole life.

They fight over Jett but other than that she adores him.

Just like I did.

My father's a powerful man, very intelligent, charming when he wants to be, rough when he needs to be, and has the confidence and courage of twenty men. Some of it born, some of it taught, the rest of it earned.

As she finishes fake griping on a lovely smile, I reach over and take her hand. "Mom."

Her eyes flicker as she takes in my sober expression. "What is it, Jaxson? What's wrong?" Her free hand trembles up to her mouth. "Oh dear God. It's Jett, isn't it? He's hurt!"

"No. Jett's fine, Mom."

"Jeremy!?" She steps closer, searching my eyes with fear in hers. Jeremy is in the Marines and she has reason to think my expression is because I got bad news. "Please tell me he's okay!"

I pull her into my arms, crushing her to me, choked up as I reassure her, "Jeremy's okay, Mom. I'm sorry. He's okay."

"What is it?" she whispers into my chest.

I am fucking dying over this. Pain is streaking through my body and I can't even speak.

A door closes in the distance and I stiffen. Only one person has the key.

Congressman Michael Cocker walks into the kitchen and takes one look at us, guessing I've already told her. He's stunned to see me here and his façade of self-control vanishes as his stern lips go soft, his jaw lax, green eyes narrowing in horror.

"Michael!" Mom cries out. "Jaxson was just about to tell me some bad news. Look at his face. He's a mess. Don't worry. It's not the boys. Everyone's okay."

Dad and I stare at each other. His eyes darken as his jaw ticks. "I see. What were you going to say, Jaxson?"

Images of him in the waiting room, stiffly talking to Rachel, nodding to Ellen, revealing just how deep the affair went for him, slam into my mind. My teeth grit together.

"Jaxson, tell us!" Mom demands.

My eyes are still locked on Dad's. "Can I talk to you

alone?" He nods and against Mom's angry objections, we walk into the backyard past the fountain for privacy. The moon is only a sliver tonight so she can't see us well.

"Mom's watching from the kitchen window," my father mutters, glancing back, facial muscles tight.

"You tell her, or I will."

His head slowly turns. "What is that going to do but bring her pain?" He looks desperate for me to understand.

"She thinks Ellen Sawyer didn't like her opinions at the Women's Club, Dad! There were six people there today who know something Mom doesn't. Do you think that's fair?"

He steps closer. "Jaxson, is it fair that I fell in love with someone else? No. It's not fair to a lot of people. Ellen and I were—"

"—I don't want to hear you say her name!"

"If your plan here is to uproot your mother's whole world, listen for *her.*"

My father's face is rarely soft. Can't remember a time it ever was, frankly. But right now as he looks into my eyes, he's vulnerable.

I have the power to take everything from him. There is a certain satisfaction in that. "You mean for you. You're trying to protect your ass."

"Jaxson, please look at me like a man and not your

father." I blink at that and seeing I'm listening, he continues, "Your mother and I got married very young and she was very different from what I thought I wanted. She was sweet, innocent and good. I had fire in my blood and I was a rebel by nature. It's where you boys get that from. We were opposites. It's what drew us together but it almost tore us apart, too. We never fought. And to my stupid young self that meant there was no passion."

I cross my arms, listening.

"Ellen. She swore and drank and smoked and laughed loudly. She was a lady, don't get me wrong. But she rode that fine line only a lady can. I saw how you felt about Rachel today. It can't be too hard for you to understand how I was drawn to her mother. I fell in love with Ellen, but now I know I wouldn't have been happy with her. It was passionate, yes, but that kind of passion often comes with fights. I thought I wanted that but it would have been a hard road, which I couldn't see until I was on it. It's why she chose John and I chose your mother. We *chose* them. We could have chosen each other." Off my look, he explains, "I love Nancy. You know I do. And I love you boys more than I love anything."

"So you want me not to tell her so you can keep her."

"Yes! And to keep her safe. It was over two decades ago, Jaxson! Do you know much this would hurt her, and it's

215

not even happening now? All the memories would be tainted. What you're feeling now, and what I've carried in me, is terrible! Do you want your mother to feel this?"

I hang my head, looking at him under my eyebrows. "You want me to believe Mrs. Sawyer was the only one?"

Dad huffs through his nose. "Yes! This wasn't the act of a man who loves being unfaithful. I hated it when it was happening. It was a love affair and I was a kid." Shaking his head at the memory, he confesses, "I have never touched another woman since. The idea is abhorrent to me." He runs his hands through his greying dark-blonde hair. "I knew if I told her, the family would tear apart. We need each other. You boys need us as much as we need you. Don't take this from everyone for something that died over twenty years ago!"

We stare at each other. I can hear his logic. I know my brothers. They would be wrecked. Everything would collapse. Struggling, I grate, "I'm going to leave it up to you, Dad. But I have lost respect for you today. And there's only one way you can win that back."

His face contorts with anger, pride and pain. "Don't make me choose between your respect or your mother's."

Through gritted teeth, I tell him, "I believe in loyalty, Dad. You taught me that and now it means nothing."

"I have been loyal for over twenty years! And that I

taught you boys that is the greatest achievement of my life. If you want to hate me for this, I can't stop you. But if I had told you boys, and tore apart this family, you wouldn't have become the men that you are."

Shaking my head in my painful resistance, I turn on my heel and leave him there with his demons.

Inside, Mom is waiting and she won't be ignored. "What is going on?!"

"Mom."

"No, Jaxson! Tell me this instant what the hell is going on!"

I meet her eyes and hold them. My throat gets tight and I whisper, "Rachel's pregnant."

Mom steps back, her hands rushing to cover her mouth. "It's yours?"

I don't know why I say it, but I do. "Yes."

29

RACHEL

Two weeks later.

"Hey Roomie!" Sylvia sings as she returns from Trader Joes.

"I'm in my new office slash bedroom!" I call back, tapping away on the keyboard. I don't look up as she pokes her head in. "Almost done with this chapter."

"Well, I got you some soda water. How're you feeling?"

"Better today. Think that part is over," I mutter from my story of how in Peru's jungle we saw a snake so big it could have starred in the movie Anaconda. "Let me just finish up and I'll come out, okay?"

"Sure thing!" She hums her way to her kitchen, then

shouts, "Did you see who called?"

My fingers freeze over the keys. "No. Who?"

"Ryan."

"Oh." With my shoulders straightening again I keep right on working. "Probably wants money for some bill."

"He probably wants to know if you're ready for that test," she calls back.

God. Eleven weeks along now. That test is scarier than an impending IRS audit.

Rolling my eyes, I shout, "I told him I'm waiting until the twelfth week so he can wait with me." I pause. "Well not *with* me, but...you know."

She chuckles. "You're handling this so well!"

What choice do I have? Ever since returning to New York the strength I thought I had when I was with Jaxson has waned with each passing day.

But I don't want anyone poking me with needles until I'm damn good and ready.

I won't harm this baby just because Ryan is impatient. Which is what I told him last time we fought.

It's not only that, though.

I don't want to find out it's his.

Muttering to myself, "Shit. Lost my focus," I save the Microsoft Word document and gently shut the slender lid of my MacBook Air, pushing away from my best friend's loaner desk so I can see what she's up to.

Sylvia holds up dark chocolate covered caramels. "Who loves you?"

"Oh my God. Give me those." She tosses the clear plastic box to me and I barely catch it. "Oof."

She laughs and keeps tucking everything she's bought into its proper cabinet or fridge shelf. "I had an offer to open a second boutique in SoHo today."

"You did? That's amazing!" I rip off the plastic. "Partners, or what?"

"The guys who own Travesty."

"That little shop on Seventh?"

"Mmhmm. Just men's clothes and they want to branch out. So they thought we could go in together and have a two-fer-one location. Isn't that a great idea?"

"I love it," I smile while chewing.

She cocks an eyebrow at me. "You love the idea or the chocolate caramels?"

"Chocolate caramels," I smirk and shake my head. "The idea! It's really great. You going to do it?"

"I'm having a lawyer look at the proposal. Thought Ryan might help me out." Off my look, she explodes, "I'm kidding!! Ha! You should see your face. Like I'd ever do that."

As she folds the bags and tucks them beside her

refrigerator, she asks the million-dollar question, "Have you heard from Jaxson?"

"You think I wouldn't have told you the second you walked in the door?" I smile. "No. Nothing."

"You could call him."

"And say what, Sylvia? I miss you?"

On a sad smile she lays out her worries. "Honey, you haven't gone anywhere. You just stay in that room writing that damn book. Maybe you should call him and tell him you miss him. Maybe that will free you up. Get it out there." She flings her arms out like she's shooing away bad energy. "Just open the windows a bit, you know?"

"I have gone outside. When you're off working, I sometimes get coffee down the street. I've been to Central Park twice to clear my head."

"And?"

And New York doesn't feel like it used to.

Up until recently it's been home to me even inside my heart. I loved the electricity of it, mostly, and I guess the status, too. Now it just feels congested and smoggy and dirty and…lonely.

"And…I'm not calling him. There's so much going on, Sylvia."

She lands her hands on the counter and sighs. "I know. If I were in your shoes, I'd do exactly the same thing.

221

Just hole up and wait. I don't blame you. But watching from my vantage point is stressing me the fuck out!" Flipping around, she opens the fridge. "I know you can't, but I'm going to have a glass of wine." As she reaches for a glass, she throws up a hand. "I want to call Ryan myself and tell him to cool his heels!"

My smile contorts as an odd ache pierces me. "Ouch!" I double over as it grows stronger.

"What's wrong?" She rushes around the counter and lays a gentle hand on my back.

"Ow. I feel...I feel..."

"Rachel?!"

I've stood up but I don't know it.

"Rachel!"

I blink to Sylvia and see her pointing at the chair. There's blood on it. "Nooooo," I whisper, running to the bathroom with her right behind me.

She sits on the floor by the toilet, her hand on my trembling legs while I cry over my lost child.

As time slowly passes I slip into numbness.

She wets tissues and dabs my face, then turns on the shower. "You rinse off, honey," she whispers.

When I finally twist the shower faucet off, she is there with a towel and a robe over her arm. She wraps me in it and leads me into her living room.

"I want to lie down," I quietly moan.

"Uh uh," she whispers with a firm headshake. "You'll just cry in there alone. I cancelled my date with Henry. You and I are gonna have lots of wine, lots of chocolate, and watch anything on TV you want. Or we can just sit here and talk, or say nothing at all. But I'm staying with you and you're staying out here with me. You're not alone tonight, honey."

Sniffling I nod and bury my head in her shoulder. She wraps me up in a big hug while I sob. "I wanted the baby," I whisper into her curly hair.

"I know you did," she whispers. "But this one wasn't meant to be."

30

JAXSON

Just after eleven o'clock p.m. I wake up covered in sweat, panting from a dream I had where Rachel was crying. I could hear her but I couldn't find her. I searched, calling out her name, but it was like she couldn't hear me. Just the same anguished sobs that never stopped. It was fucking torture for me.

Throwing the blanket off me I rush downstairs, completely missing the last stair altogether.

Where the fuck did I leave my phone?

Searching for it feels like searching for her in the dream and I become frantic.

"Fuck. This. Shit."

After I tear my house apart, I find the damn thing in the barn on top of the milk tank. Running a hand through my hair I do what I should have done two weeks ago.

Rachel picks up, her voice quiet. "Hello?"

"Rach, it's me. I'm sorry I took so long to call you. I need to see you." At her silence, I start stammering, "Look, I don't give a shit if he's in the other room or even in the bed right next to you, you're mine and I fucked up letting you leave like that. I'm coming to New York. If you don't tell me where you live, I'll tear my hair out. Just give me two minutes of your time. That's all I need."

"This isn't Rachel," the woman says, her voice still quiet. "This is Sylvia."

I blink rapidly at the wall searching for comprehension. Waking up like that has my brain completely sideways. "Wait. Who are you? Do I have the wrong number?"

She whispers, "Hang on." I hear some rummaging and then a few seconds of my impatience later, she says in a louder voice. "I had to get to my room."

"What the fuck? Who is this?"

"I'm Rachel's best friend, Jaxson. This is her phone. She's sleeping on the couch."

Oh. Sylvia. Right. She told me about her, but I wasn't expecting...

"Let me talk to her."

"Jaxson," she begins, her voice somber. "She's living

with me now. They split up right after she got back."

My heart starts pounding even harder.

Why didn't she call me?

Does she not want me?

Holy shit.

How did I fuck this up this badly?

Pain is tearing my stomach apart. "But you're talking to me, so that must mean I have a chance."

"Jaxson, she lost the baby tonight."

My heart stops.

The dream.

The sobs.

My chest knots up and I groan, "Where do you live?"

31

JAXSON

At three o'clock the next day, cabs at JFK line up twelve deep so it isn't long before I'm climbing in saying, "West Village." The driver nods. He doesn't ask for the exact address until we cross into Manhattan.

Just like in the movies I've seen by the director Edward Burns, a line of brownstone apartments take up both sides of the entire tree-shaded street the cab pulls onto and parks on.

I don't like admitting it but it's charming and homey, despite being in a metropolis.

There's more pedestrian action than in Atlanta, and infinitely more than at my quiet ranch. Loads of people are walking their dogs, carrying yoga mats while talking on cell phones, or heading who knows where to with coffees in their hands and dressed in clothes like Rachel wears. And that fucking douche bag she was with.

It's gnawing at me.

She didn't call me when they split.

It's this town that has her.

How can I compete with New York City?

Fuck it.

I have to try.

I've been dying inside.

Paying the man I step outside with my eyes locked on the second story window. After searching random corners I manage to dislodge six pebbles, bouncing them in my palm before I aim for the glass.

One. Then two. Then three.

It feels like a pro boxer's using my heart as a punching bag, but the second I see her poke her head out the window, I feel instantly better.

I have to make this right.

"Jaxson?!"

"Hey!" I call up through a cupped hand. "Wanna climb an oak tree?"

Her pink lips slowly spread in a smile and she nods with both hands on the windowsill. "Yes, please."

"I'm comin' up!" Through the glass in the door I see a pretty black woman coming down the staircase inside. She gives me a big smile as she lets me in. "You must be Sylvia."

Eying me with curiosity from head to toe, she nods. "And you must be Jaxson Cocker. Nice to meet you. You came quickly."

"Something no man wants to hear," I smirk.

"I like you." She wags a finger on her way to the street. "I'm going to give you some privacy." Smiling with self-satisfaction she heads off.

I sprint upstairs and don't even knock. Rachel jumps back, yelping.

I cock an eyebrow at her. "Waiting for me to knock before you opened it?"

"Maybe," she smiles, but her face looks like she's been crying all day. I'm sure she has.

"Come here." I pull her into my arms. The façade of levity evaporates as Rachel starts weeping. I slowly rock her grief-stricken body and she goes completely limp in my protective embrace. "I've got you, baby. I've got you."

"Why are you here? Sylvia called you?" she croaks.

Against her head I whisper, "No, I called you last night. She answered and told me what happened."

Burrowing into my shoulder, Rachel whimpers. "I wanted the baby, Jaxson. And it was so awful." She chokes, "I felt empty! People say, *Oh, I had a miscarriage* and other people say, *Oh, are you going to try again?* But what about *that*

229

baby? There was a little child inside me and now it's gone! It's just gone!"

"I know, Rach, I'm so sorry." I edge her inside, kick the door shut and pick her up to carry her to the couch. Kneeling in front of her I push dampened hair away from her wet cheeks.

I want to turn back time and go through it with her. But since I can't, I know only two ways to take away those tears – piss her off or make her laugh.

"Rach, I know why this has happened."

"Because the baby was under so much stress?" she whispers, eyes huge with guilt-laden grief. "It's my fault, isn't it? It's because of what we went through and because I was…" She chokes up.

Fuck, I've missed this face.

Completely serious, I tell her, "Because it wasn't mine. If that were my kid it would have been doing pushups in there. Especially if it was a girl."

She stares at me, then starts laughing. "Jaxson, you're so cocky, I swear. Where do you get that stuff?"

My eyes widen with mock-surprise. "What? It's true! *My* baby would have lifted you up and carried you into the delivery room. *Hey Mom, I'm here! Let's get the ball rolling!*"

Laughing, "You're insane," she covers her face like she's not allowed to let the pain go.

"Can't teach a very handsome dog new tricks, lady."

Rachel's body crumbles into laughter but new tears come. "Oh my God, Jaxson I'm so glad you're here. I can't believe Sylvia didn't tell me you were coming."

I wipe a fresh tear from her cheek with my thumb. "She said you were staying with her now. That was all I needed to know. I booked the first flight I could get." Staring at her, I need to ask the question that's been haunting me. "Rach, why didn't you call me when you broke up with your boyfriend?"

Frowning, she whispers, "I wanted to. I needed to know who was the father."

As my face contorts, I say, "I don't understand. You wanted to give it another try with him if it was his, or what?"

She blinks at me like I've just spoken another language. "What? No! Because why would you want to raise another man's baby?"

Gripping her hands, my voice is thick. "Are you kidding me?! I've been a fucking mess since you left. That's what you needed to hear from me? I would have raised that baby no matter whose it was if you wanted me there. Hell, I was ready to kick Ryan's ass if you told me it was okay!" Seeing her surprised expression, I groan, "That's not what stopped me from calling you. I didn't think I had anything to offer you, out on a ranch in the middle of nowhere!"

"Jaxson," she whispers.

"Wait. Just hold on. I didn't think I had anything to give you, that I'd lost you to this city. But I have *me*, Rachel, I can give you me."

Her breath hitches, but I'm not done pouring my guts out to her. I have to convince her to be with me. I will never be happy without her.

"Rachel, listen to me. I've never needed anyone, but I need you. And if you'll give me the chance I'll do everything in my power to make you smile every fucking day of your life."

Her pink lips tremble open.

But before she can turn me down and tell me how great New York Fucking City is, I quickly continue, "Look. I was thinking you could come live with me half the month, then come back here the other half so you're not bored out of your mind. I can't come with you here. The animals need me and the farm can't run without me at the helm. I've got someone watching it now while I'm gone but I can't do that every month. I've considered selling it—"

"—Jaxson, you can't sell your ranch," she quietly interrupts.

"I know," I groan, dipping my head. "It's a part of me. But so are you. I don't want to live without you. Is there any way you could split the time, and write from there? And when they fly you to places for your books... Atlanta has one of the biggest airports in America!"

She squeezes my hands, frowning like it's too complicated or something. "That sounds—"

"—I don't care. I love you, Rachel."

She gasps and stares at me in wonder. "You do?" she whispers.

"I've loved you since I was eight." I pull her to me and kiss her, picking her up off the couch and holding her so that her legs are dangling. She laughs as I kiss all over her face.

When I can't wait for an answer any longer, I search her eyes and whisper, "Will you do it?"

A happy smile and bright blue eyes are staring at me. "I love you, too, Jaxson. But you always knew I did."

Overwhelmed because that sounds like a yes to me, tears cloud my vision.

These tears are strong.

Filled with amazement that I could be so lucky.

That I found my soul mate when I was just a boy.

That even though she was taken from me, I was given a second chance at happiness.

A chance to make her mine.

"You'll do it then?"

"No, you crazy man. I won't split my time." My heart stops. "I want to live with you in Georgia. All the time."

A grin quickly spreads and I shout, "Holy shit! Are you serious!"

"I am," she smiles. "I love your home. I won't be bored. Please take me with you. I want to be with you."

Those are words I never thought I'd hear. I spin her around and shout something incoherent, but then realize what I'm doing. Setting her quickly down I lay my palm on her abdomen, "You alright? Shouldn't have spun you around like that."

Rachel covers my hand with hers, smiling gently. "God, I love you."

Taking her beautiful face in my hands I kiss her and she laces her fingers into my hair. Against her lips, I whisper, "I love you, too, baby. Get ready to be made very happy."

"Too late. You already did it," she whispers back.

I crush her in a deep kiss. We've missed each other so much it grows heated and I have to force myself to stop. "Whoa whoa. Give you a few days to heal. I'm going to take you home, rest you up, then I'm going to fuck the ever living shit out of you."

Rachel grins, "Ooooo, I like the dirty talk."

"I'm just getting started," I smirk and rest my forehead to hers. "Rachel Sawyer…I love you."

She teases in a whisper, "Took you long enough to tell me."

Gazing at her, I kiss her nose. "Never gonna make that mistake again. I love you. There, see?"

32

RACHEL

As Jaxson sets my two suitcases down inside near the door, I walk around his farmhouse with new eyes.

It's my home now.

He stayed five nights with me in New York to help me take care of things, and sew up my old life before we flew here.

I introduced him to some of my favorite restaurants in between doing mundane things like changing my address with the post office, going to the dry cleaner to pick up articles of clothing I wasn't willing to leave behind, and to my storage unit. We tore through that together and sent my personal items and keepsakes here via U.P.S. — they'll be coming soon. I signed a form giving the storage company permission to auction off the rest of my unit.

My best friend got a chance to spend some time with Jaxson over wine and pizza the three of us shared last night, sitting around her coffee table. It was my mini going away party, she said.

She asked Jaxson a lot of questions about his ranch and he answered her with happiness lighting his eyes. I filled in what he left out, like how he touches each of his cows in the mornings as they head out to graze and how some of them have very distinct, social personalities.

Though my leaving the city saddened her, she confessed to me, "When he called you that night I guessed it was probably going to happen. I knew you weren't happy in New York anymore."

When Jaxson excused himself to use the bathroom she and I watched him walk away. He glanced over his shoulder. "Are you ladies checking out my ass?"

We grinned and Sylvia wagged her finger at him. "I like you." As soon as the door shut, she whispered to me, "I'm so happy for you, honey."

I hugged her and whispered back, "Thank you for letting me stay here."

Now I'm in Georgia. I can't believe this is where I live. And that I'm with him, the boy I'd follow anywhere.

Jaxson is standing by the door, watching with his thumbs in his belt loops.

I smile over my shoulder, "Home."

He shakes his head like he can't believe it either, and crosses to join me in front of the fireplace, pulling me close.

"Where do you want the desk?"

"Ooooo, I get a desk?"

He laughs. "I'm guessing you can't be a writer without one."

"Over there!" I point to where the dining table is. "You always eat on the porch anyway."

"Done." His hands travel down my body. "This dress has gotta go."

I whisper against his smile, "I hate it anyway," raising my arms over my head.

He slips it off and drinks in my body with his emerald eyes. Leaning in he kisses the soft mounds above my bra as he reaches around to snap it off. Freeing me he takes me in his hands, gently biting my right nipple.

"Got to make better use of that table while it's still got the view," he murmurs, carrying me to it, shoving one of the chairs out of the way with his boot as he sets me down. Hesitating, he asks, "How're you feelin'? You want to wait longer, baby?"

I shake my head a little. "I just want you closer. And I need you."

We kiss for a very long time, like we did the nights we

slept in Sylvia's guest bed while he let me heal. He's been so ginger with me, so kind. But I have been aching for him ever since I left Georgia. Some might say I need more healing time but the connection you feel with the man you love, like how deeply I love Jaxson, can only truly be expressed one way. It's the binding of our bodies that communicates the bond of our souls.

He pulls his shirt off and groans as I kiss his nipples and then press my lips down his ribs and over his abs. My hand searches and discovers him erect and straining to be free of these jeans.

In the most tantalizing way I unzip them while I hold his eyes. He's gazing back at me with love-laced hunger as he unbuckles his belt and throws it aside, cocking an eyebrow at me like he's a stripper. I quietly laugh and motion with a glance for him to take off my panties.

"Don't mind if I do." He lifts me up to tug them down my legs, bringing them to his nose for a second while holding my eyes. "Yummy," he smirks.

"Oh my God, stop."

He laughs and tosses them onto the floor before sliding his jeans down and off, his cock now unhindered.

"No boxers?" I smile, taking his veiny length in my hand as a heated need pools out between my thighs. I'm aching and ready. His eyes go hooded with pleasure as I stroke him.

"Didn't pack enough. Had no clue how long I'd be in New York."

New York...

It'll only be a memory now.

I won't have to go back if I don't want to. Everything can be done online. I don't even have to tell my publisher I moved...but I will. Just not yet.

Tonight is for us.

Jaxson pulls my body closer to the table's edge and claims my mouth in a hot kiss that sends shivers into my skin. He bends at the knees to enter me and hovers his blunt tip just against my moistness. He searches my eyes and says, "I want you to be my wife."

My breath hitches in surprise and I whisper, "Really, Jaxson?"

He slides into me one inch at time as his murmurs against my lips, "Will you marry me, Rachel Sawyer?"

On a moan, I tease him, "Aren't you supposed to be on one knee?"

"Who says?" He reaches the deepest point in me and stares into my eyes. "Marry me."

Of course Jaxson Cocker wouldn't propose the way it's 'supposed to be done.' He moves in the opposite direction of the masses and always has. It's one of the things

I've adored about him. I followed him as a child because he was a rebel and didn't think like anyone else. And now I'll follow him as a woman. And while both of us are grown, neither have really changed. Not where it counts.

I lace my fingers into his thick sandy-brown hair, the same color as mine, and whisper, "I would love to be your wife, Jaxson."

He kisses me. "I love you." I'm about to respond but he starts to move and my soft body melts into the hardness of him. The pain of what we've gone through to get here pushes at my psyche and I need to let it go. So I press my breasts into Jaxson's naked chest, look up at him, and whisper an urgent, "Harder."

He groans this wonderfully sexy man-moan and starts working, lifting me off the table and hooking my legs around his ass. I grip onto his shoulders. His thick fingers dig into me, holding me up, and we fuck like this in front of the windows in the waning light of evening. Our breaths combine. Our tongue lace. Our hearts start beating in rhythm with each other because we've found home.

Jaxson and I cum together, the air vibrating with my loud moans and his free roar.

He's all mine.

And I am his.

33

JAXSON

We've been in bed for days. The only time we've gotten up is to refuel with some home-cooked meals, milk the cows and collect eggs. Oh, and I had to go out when the guys came to pick up their collection. Rachel asked if we could get some of the cheese they made, back. The guys agreed with smiling faces, mostly because they were happy for us.

"Found yourself a girlfriend, huh Jax?"

"Fiancé."

"No shit?!"

Rachel just grinned. I think she's still letting this all soak in.

Me? I'm loving every minute. Those two weeks without her were the loneliest of my life.

I'm ready for this.

She's lying next to me, her naked body half-covered by the blanket as she watches me read from her laptop.

"Well?"

"It's really good, Rach."

"Yeah?"

I nod, still absorbed in the story of Peru. The way she's described it in her book, the journey from the airport was crazy but other than that, it feels peaceful. "This is what they do at retreats?" I mutter, lost in the images her story has laid out for me.

"It was so lovely, Jaxson. I tried to do it justice but it's hard to."

"No." I glance to her. "I can see it in my mind. You've done a really great job evoking the feelings of the environment. And I'm jealous you saw that snake."

"It was terrifying!"

"I know. I want to see it."

"You're crazy," she laughs. "Oh my God, I remember you used to like snakes!"

Smiling at her from the corner of my eyes I nod. "They're very cool. I see 'em up here sometimes." Her face goes serious, and I laugh. "You're still afraid of them."

Closing the computer I set it down on the nightstand and stare at the darkened fireplace.

"You're thinking you want to go to Peru, huh," she smiles, poking my side a few times. "I'm that good, aren't I?"

Chuckling I grab her hand and squeeze it backwards until she has to bend her whole body, and yelp.

"I've always been stronger than you so just quit fighting it."

"Okay! Okay!" She's laughing and tugging away, but I pull her toward me instead, rolling on top of her.

"Okay what?"

She makes an expression like she doesn't know how to answer. "Okay jerk face?"

A grin flashes on me, but I shut it down fast and say very seriously, "Okay what?"

"Okay poop head?"

Laughing, I kiss her. "Okay, Master."

"Yeah, right!" she cries out. "I'm not calling you Master!"

Tickling her I show no mercy. She's laughing and screaming and finally calls out, "Master! Okay *Master*! Stop it!!"

A text beep sounds downstairs and then the phone rings right on its tail. We both stop and listen to it. "It's yours," I say, rolling off of her.

Her publisher was going to call. She plans to ask for two more weeks to finish the final edit on her Peru book.

She leaps off the bed and runs downstairs naked. After a moment I hear her shout, "Jaxson!"

I fly down to her, protective and worried. "What?! What's up?"

She holds up the phone and shows me a text message:

Rachel, it's Cora. Remember me? From Trinity? I ran into your mom at the Women's Club. Wanted to reach out and say hi.

Crossing my arms and cocking my eyebrows I mutter, "Tell her you're looking at my cock right now."

Rachel cracks up. "Yeah, I'll do that. Let me just start typing." She fake-types and hits a fake send, her gestures big and animated. Staring at the phone, her grins falters. "What do I do?"

"What do you want to do?"

On a shrug, her face is unsure. "I'll call Jennifer back first." As she waits for her publisher to answer, Rachel comes to rest her hand around my hip, squeezing gently. "Hello Jenn! It's me. Listen, can I have a couple more weeks on the book. I'm almost done, and I just had a friend give me the thumbs up that it's good." She smiles at me and I wink back. "Yeah? Thank you. Sorry for the delay. I kinda moved to Georgia."

I can hear a woman say, "WHAT?!"

Kissing Rachel's head I walk to the kitchen so she can

take care of this. On the side of my counter is a small box where I keep odds and ends like rubber bands, zip ties, business cards and a couple pens. There are some pennies in there, too. As I start to wash the dishes we used last, I glance to it and see Mr. Jarvis's card lying on top.

I stare at it and cock my head.

The dishes get put on hold again as I turn and lean against the counter, watching Rachel, naked and sitting on my couch. She's concentrating on what her publisher is telling her about how they'll move forward with their partnership now, her fingers fiddling with the threads at the end of the throw blanket.

Hanging up she glances over. "Have you been watching me this whole time?"

"I've got an idea."

"What is it?"

Pushing off the counter I pluck out Jarvis's card and stroll over to her. "Remember the man who wanted to buy my land?"

"Of course," she says, eyes curious.

"I don't want a women's center."

"Okay." She tilts her head, wondering if I'm saying they're not needed. I can see her feminism hackles rising with each step I take toward her.

"What about a retreat? For men *and* women. Guys

246

need a place to go, too."

Rachel blinks and sits on her knees, tossing the blanket threads away. "Go on."

"What about we section off a piece of this property for a retreat that you could run."

Her soft lips part. "Are you serious?"

Starting to feel excited I plant my bare feet firmly on the hardwood and splay my hands out to paint the picture for her. "Okay, now hear me out. And stop looking at my cock."

She makes a face, trying not to smile. "Kinda hard to miss the elephant trunk, baby."

I break out laughing, but quickly force myself to be serious so I can explain the best idea I've ever had, save for asking her to be my wife.

"That far end of acreage where the fences are kinda wonky and it's not quite squared off? I can cut a path there for a driveway, quarter that off with enough land for a retreat of say, no more than ten people. Build a farmhouse like this one with bedrooms on the second floor — they can't be too big —"

"—They don't need to be!" she excitedly interrupts. "The rooms are always small. It's about the yoga and healthy eating. And massages."

"Great! Now, stop bouncing because your tits look amazing and I'm trying to focus here."

Rachel laughs and stops, covering herself with the throw blanket.

"Now now. Let's not get crazy." I point at it, and she ditches the blanket. Staring at her beautiful naked curves I nod, "That's better. Anyway, the bottom floor will have an open space like this one with folding chairs and tables against the walls that people can bring out after classes for dining and any of those journaling exercises you wrote about. We'll provide whatever you think they need, based on your own opinions and experience. You said you liked the juicing but not the raw foods. DONE. Whatever you want it to be, we can do it. Make it anything you want."

Rachel is staring at me like I'm her hero.

It feels really good.

But then she frowns, "But who would come?"

I have the answer but fuck it. I love to mess with her. It's too easy and I enjoy it too much.

Like the wind left my sail I drop my arms. "Oh shit. I didn't think of that. No one. Nobody wants to come all the way out here."

"Well, maybe if we advertised?" she offers, but I can tell she's trying to make me feel better more than save the idea, because she doesn't see how to make this happen.

"Nah. It wouldn't work."

"I'm sorry, Jaxson. It's a good idea."

I walk over to look out one of the windows, laying my palm high on the frame. My legs are staggered and I know from behind I look pretty damn good in this posture. "How's my ass looking?" I look over my shoulder and wink.

Rachel blinks at me, confused at the change of tone and subject. "Your ass looks ridiculous. You're like the statue of David, but… Oh! You're messing with me!!"

Laughing I walk back and tell her, "Rachel, Hollywood is taking over Atlanta. People are flying in from all over to work on movies and television shows. There are so many people who would drive an hour to get away from it all after filming ends. During hiatus. Hell, just for a weekend. And those people love juicing and retreats and all that yoga shit."

"How do you know all this?" she asks, smiling like I'm some sort of dumb cowboy.

"Baby, I read."

Laughing, Rachel stands up and walks to me, her breasts jiggling with each step. Not to mention that trimmed little bush of hers. Fuck.

"Oh, you read do you?"

"I sure the fuck do. Ask Mrs. Connelly," I murmur, pulling my woman to me and running my hands down her sides until they've got a firm grip on her hot ass. "Mmm…can't get enough of this."

She kisses me long and slow, rising up on her tiptoes.

"Let's do the retreat."

"Tell me you think I'm amazing," I smile down at her.

"I think you're a jerk," she whispers, kissing me.

"That'll do."

34

RACHEL

I was feeling tired so Jaxson went down to milk the cows without me this morning.

There's been a lot of change.

I've taken quiet, private moments on his property to mourn my lost pregnancy, because even though losing it means I never have to talk to Ryan again, I wanted that child.

But I've learned through the retreats I've gone to and the journaling we've done that loss must be grieved.

It can be the loss of a job, a marriage, a baby, or a dream. There are so many things we have to let go of, things that weren't meant for us or things that just go away for no reason.

But they had a place in our hearts and that hole they leave behind has to be honored.

251

I wrote a letter to my lost baby, to the child, teenager and adult it would have become. I wrote how much I loved it and would have cherished teaching it the ways of our weird world. I carried the letter with me for the past three weeks here.

Then yesterday I asked Jaxson if there was a safe place I could burn it.

To burn is to cleanse and set free.

Ashes to ashes.

Dust to dust.

So that new growth can happen.

He brought me a stainless steel bucket and left me to be alone with what I had to do.

As I held my letter, I looked up at the sky. "Sweet baby, thank you for bringing Jaxson and I together. If I hadn't come here for his help, we might not be here now. I hope I didn't do anything to make you go away from me. I know you were just a peanut, but I love you."

I burned the letter then, lit a match to its corners and held on until I couldn't anymore, watching it float into the tunnel of steel where the flames turned the letter into grey ash. Then I whispered a last, "Goodbye," and walked away.

When I came back later, Jaxson had already taken care of it for me. The bucket was clean and hanging from its hook. There was something freeing looking at it like that.

I finally let go.

As I lie here and listen to the distant sounds of my future husband making breakfast downstairs, I snuggle into the covers and gaze at my computer on his nightstand. I hit send last week. My book is now out of my hands. If people like it isn't up to me.

Footsteps pad up and I rise up on my elbow to welcome him. As he appears in his old jeans and no shirt, holding a tray of oatmeal, crispy bacon and poached eggs, I smile, "Hello."

"Hello baby," he smiles, his green eyes happy. "Feel more rested now?" Setting down the tray, he sits on the bed and hands me a coffee.

I hold it in both hands, loving the warmth of the ceramic cup. "Yes, thank you for letting me sleep in."

"You want to go into town today?"

"Why?"

He chuckles. "I've converted the city girl!"

Smiling, I take a sip. "You sure have. Why do you want to go in?"

"Thought you might need a ring for that finger." He reaches over and touches it.

"I was hoping for a desk," I frown.

His eyebrows go up. "Really? Well, we can do that instead. I know a great place. I just thought…"

"I'm just kidding," I laugh, rising up to kiss him and say, "I got you, Jaxson!"

"No, you didn't," he smirks, pushing hair back from my face.

"Yes, I did."

"No, you really didn't."

Sitting on my heels, I demand, "What do you mean?"

"I got *you*. I already bought you a damn desk. I was just playing along so you could think you're smarter than me." He sticks his tongue out. "So there."

"Shut up!" I cry out my mouth wide open in disbelief. He shoves a piece of toast in in. Like the whole piece. Mouth stuffed I smack his chest as he starts laughing.

"That'll teach you to talk back to me."

I chew fast so I can send a retort.

"Uh uh," he mutters. "No talking back to your sugar daddy."

Man is it hard to swallow this much toast! As soon as I get it down, I bark at him, "I have money!"

He tackles me. "Then give it to me!" Pinning my arms with his hands he sits on my hips. "Shhhh...I like you quiet and struggling."

"Stop it, Jaxson!"

He kisses me quiet. The kisses grow and soon those jeans are gone and he's spreading my legs with his knees, plunging that gorgeous cock inside me, "Beg me to stop."

"I don't want you to stop," I moan.

He nuzzles my neck and murmurs in my ear, "You always tell me, *stop it, Jaxson!* Don't you want me to stop fucking you like this?"

"Uh uh. Don't stop." He's so good, working those hips and filling me completely with each stroke.

"Too bad. I'm stopping." He pulls out abruptly.

"No!"

Laughing, he flips me over like I weigh less than tissue paper. He grabs my ass and slams his cocks in my pussy from behind, making me absolutely purr.

"Fuck, your pussy feels so good, baby," Jaxson growls, pinching my ass cheek and throwing shivers into me from the pleasure of it. He moves in a rhythm that drives me out of my mind with tingles, burning and aching for it to last. His cock is at its hardest and I'm so wet that it's sliding in and out of me in the most delicious way.

"Ohhhh," I moan, gripping the pillows.

"Grab the headboard," he groans. "Hold on for your life."

I claw up it to grip the wood as tightly as I can.

Jaxson sets his foot on the bed, balancing his weight on both it and his other knee.

His hips start to move, and he's fucking me so slowly

that I have to wonder why he told me to grip this thing.

Not that I'm complaining.

Each slow and sure penetration of his pulsing shaft is amazing.

He's arched my ass up with his hands, kneading the soft flesh and groaning that deep masculine sound of intense pleasure.

I love how this feels.

The sweet burn starts to build in my core, drawn out with his skill.

But then as I start moaning with an impending orgasm he picks up the speed while maintaining this rhythm that is driving me insane.

I go to cry out and yelp and he moves faster, his girth widening and stretching me as he nears the edge, too.

Suddenly I'm cumming and he is fucking me harder until I start to scream from how good it feels.

Jaxson's cock explodes inside me, filling me until he has unleashed everything. I can't stop cumming, the walls of my pussy tremble and clench around him.

When he's satisfied I am shaking all over, making sounds I've never heard myself make, he kisses my back and thickly says, in my ear, "Gotcha, Rachel."

All I can do is whimper.

35

JAXSON

I called to gather a family BBQ at my parent's house, but I didn't say why. Mom thought she knew, so I had to gently let her down.

"No, Mom, Rachel lost the baby."

"Oh no! Oh honey, I'm so sorry."

"Don't bring it up to her, okay?"

She whispered, "Of course I won't," with that kind of voice I've only heard women use, filled with the compassion that comes from knowing what women go through. "Well, I'm looking real forward to seeing her after these years. I'll plan it. Do you want to call your brothers?"

"No, can you do it?"

"Alright. Did you ever tell them about the baby?"

I grimace and keep my voice normal, as I say, "No

Only you and Dad knew."

Only Dad knows a lot more than that.

Now Rachel has changed her clothes about twelve times and I've sat back and kept my mouth shut until she finally looked over and said, "You haven't said you like this one."

"I said I liked the last six."

Her pretty lips form a thin line. "Jaxson."

"What," I chuckle. "I'm not Ryan."

She makes a face and walks back into the bathroom. Following her, I try to turn back that moment. "Hey. Sorry."

"That wasn't nice," she whispers, slipping out of a dress that was stunning but frankly way too much for a Cocker Family BBQ.

Leaning against the doorframe I cross my arms. "Rach, if you want a man who knows fashion you'll have to ask a gay man. Like Ryan."

She stifles a smile and side-eyeballs me. "Okay, fine."

"No. No 'fine.' You love me the way I am. I love you the way you are. Now put on something less glamorous and let's go."

As I turn around she calls after me, "See! I knew you didn't like it!"

Laughing under my breath I shake my head and stroll downstairs in my dark green sweater, brown boots and blue jeans. Grabbing a bottle of wine from my cabinet I hear a beep on my phone.

There's a text message from Cora.

Jarvis tells me you have big plans. Don't cut me out of this commission.

Smirking I text back.

Never crossed my mind. It's all yours.

I hit send, calling up to Rachel, "Cora knows about the deal!"

"What'd she say?"

I turn around and have to catch my breath. Rachel is in jeans and a light blue blouse with low heels, a light jacket over her arm. Off my expression, she smiles.

We walk to each other and I kiss her lips, then her nose, then her forehead, whispering against it, "You look beautiful."

Laying her hands on my biceps, she smiles up at me. "When you said glamorous, I knew I was working too hard. See? I just needed a clue. That's why I was asking you."

Nodding, I hold her eyes. "Got it. Lesson learned."

"So, what'd Cora say?"

"She wanted to make sure I didn't leave her out of her commission."

Rachel chuckles. "Shrewd. Maybe I should call her. Might feel like home."

She means New York, but I don't like it so I firmly tell her, "This is home."

Nodding she tilts her chin for a kiss. I give her one and as she walks away, I give her ass a swift spank, "Damn you are looking fine as hell in those jeans."

She laughs and goes for her purse as I snatch up my keys from the counter, grab the wine and go to open the door for her.

36

JAXSON

Since everyone lives in town, I'm always the last to arrive at our BBQs. The front door is unlocked. Rachel and I enter my childhood home, holding hands. She points to the stairs we snuck up together as children, and her blue eyes go wide at the memory.

I kiss her fingertips and lead her through the kitchen filled with signs of a feast having been prepared toward the voices wafting in from the backyard.

"Ready?"

Rachel smiles. "It's so strange seeing this place again after all these years. Like I have new eyes."

I open the sliding glass door and everyone turns at the sound. They're all sitting at the long table set inside four poles of hanging twinkle lights, another table off to the side with homemade dishes waiting to be enjoyed, each covered in mesh tents to discourage bugs from getting there first.

The yard is long with paths leading through it to the oak tree border, and the dolphin fountain is set back and to the right.

Mom invited everyone in the family who could come, including Aunt Anna, Uncle Dave and their four kids, cousins all in similar ages as my brothers. They live in Savannah and I didn't expect to see them, but I'm very happy they're here.

Everyone walks to meet us with smiles on their faces as they glance from Rachel to our entwined fingers.

"Rachel Sawyer!" Mom gushes as she goes to hug her. "How you've grown! And you look so much like your mother did when I knew her! It's a little freaky!"

Dad and I hold a look.

He hasn't told Mom, and now is not the time for that.

"Hi Mrs. Cocker," Rachel smiles, awkward as she glances quickly to my dad. "Mr. Cocker."

"Rachel," he says with a small nod. "Good to see you again."

Fuck if this doesn't tear me up with anger.

But I conceal it and focus on the twins. "Do you guys remember Rachel? Her family lived two doors from us until I was ten."

Justin shakes her hand and says, "Of course I do."

"Liar," Jason laughs, warning her, "He's a politician Rachel. Don't believe a word he says."

"*Believe* me when I say my twin is an asshole for telling you that," Justin smirks.

"Language!" Grams shouts from her seat. She's too old to rise up for this introduction but she's watching us like a very interested, protective eagle.

Rachel chuckles and turns to Jake. "I remember you," she whispers. "Your eyes always had that smile in them, even when you were crawling."

He laughs and shakes her hand. "I wish I could say I remember. This is Drew, my wife."

The pretty brunette my brother swept off her resistant feet comes in for a hug and drawls with her southern Georgia, small town accent, "It's still strange being called his wife. So nice to meet you!"

"When did you get married?" Rachel asks.

"Just a few months ago now."

"Don!" I call out, waving him over. "Rachel this is my Uncle Don, and his wife, Aunt Marie. Did you ever meet them?"

"I don't think so."

Mom offers, "No, they never came by for dinner when you and your parents were here."

Dad and I exchange a look that nobody catches. Why would they? They're all in the dark. Rachel and I are the only ones who know what he did.

Don fills her in, "I married Marie, who's Jaxson's aunt. So I'm an in-law," he winks. "Marie and Michael are May's children." He motions to Grams who waves like, *yes, that's me.*

"Jett and Jeremy aren't here," Mom says. "Did Jaxson fill you in about his other brothers?"

"He did. Jett's traveling the states and Jeremy is in the Marines."

"That's right. But meet my sister!" Mom grabs Aunt Anna's arm and pulls her forward. "See the resemblance?" They both have very similar coloring, brown hair and eyes. "Jake there and Jeremy, my two youngest boys, inherited that."

Rachel and Aunt Anna shake hands and she introduces her husband, Uncle David before saying, "My children did, too." She points to my four well-dressed, very attractive brown-haired cousins, calling their names off in the order they're standing in. "I'm not going to overwhelm you with ages and professions, dear, but that's Jameson, Josh, Jordan, and my pride and joy, Jocelyn."

Her eyes widening, Rachel smiles, "All 'J' names!"

On a laugh, Aunt Anna explains, "Yes, my sister and I are a little competitive. And I say *pride and joy* because while she had two more children than I did, Nancy always wanted a girl and I got one."

"Stop rubbing it in," Mom grumbles, but it's all in fun. "Well, let's eat!"

I hold up my hand. "Hold on. First let me introduce her to Grams."

Handing the wine bottle to Mom, I lead Rachel over as the family remains standing with wine or cocktails in their hands, falling into easy conversations.

Grandma May Cocker eyes Rachel as we walk up. "I was here one of those nights your parents came for dinner. Your grandfather Jerald was here too, Jaxson, with me. Do you remember?"

I shake my head, "Sorry, Grams. I don't."

She waves her fragile hand. "No matter. But I remember this one! Rachel my dear, you were always a cute girl but my! You have grown into a beauty!"

Rachel is glowing as she smiles at Grams, and she leans down to give her a hug that takes my grandma by surprise. "I remember you, Mrs. Cocker." Straightening up, she points to the fountain. "You made Jaxson and Jerald— Jett —stop splashing me."

With a twinkle, Grams says, "You do remember! They terrorized you!" Her eyes drift to me. "Now I know why."

37

JAXSON

I chuckle under my breath and take Rachel's hand to call out with my calm, deep voice, "Everyone, can I get you all to shut the hell up for a second?"

Jason jokes, "What, Grams, is 'hell' not a big enough swearword?"

"I'm letting it pass," she waves with a mischievous glint in her eyes.

Mom and Aunt Marie act shocked, but everyone else is smirking or chuckling at that. I make it a point not to look at Dad. This isn't about him.

Rachel squeezes my hand and I glance to her and squeeze back.

Turning to my family, I begin, "Alright, so most of you know or have gathered that Rachel and I met when we

266

were kids. We were best friends, even if she was an icky girl."
Light laughter all around. My smile fades as I continue, "She
moved away and we didn't see each other until just a few
months ago. But I recognized her right away." I glance to
Rachel who's watching me with love in her eyes. "So I
punched her boyfriend in the face and stole her right out
from under him."

My brothers and cousins start laughing.

Jason loudly hoots through cupped hands.

I wink to Mom because her finding that address is part
of the reason I'm standing here. She shakes her head at me
like she raised bad boys. But there's pride in her eyes.

"Well, you might be wondering—"

"—Who the hell stole our silent brother and replaced
him with you? Yeah!" Justin calls out.

Laughing I shake my head. "Well, I finally have
something to say, Justin. The thing is, everyone, I want you
all to know that you just met a girl I fell in love with when I
was eight years old."

The females make *awww*-noises and some reflexively
touch their hearts.

I glance to Jason.

He nods and walks over to the food table.

Everyone watches to see what he's doing.

He reaches under the white tablecloth and produces a

long sunflower with its roots still attached.

Rachel lets go of my hand and covers her mouth in surprise.

As Jason makes his way through the crowd he's smiling at her. He hands me the flower and steps back, ignoring Justin's curious look as to why he wasn't in on this, too.

Everyone gasps as I get down on one knee.

Rachel starts shaking her head over and over, both hands covering her face.

I lay my palm out for her to hold. She slides her fingers onto mine, her other hand floating down, her blue eyes liquid now.

Holding out the sunflower, I struggle against my own rising emotions to say, "Doubt thou the stars are fire; Doubt that the sun doth move; Doubt truth to be a liar; But never doubt I love."

"Oh, Jaxson," she whispers, tears falling down her cheeks.

"Rachel Sawyer…will you marry me?"

Nodding, she answers, "Yes!"

My family riots with loud shouting and cheering, rushing forward to hug us.

Jake holds still an extra second. "You fucking outdid me, you bastard."

I laugh as we separate and Justin demands why he wasn't told. "How come you had Jason get that flower and not me?"

Cocking an eyebrow at him, I ask, "You really think you're a romantic? Jason practically fell over himself to help me out. You would have given me shit."

"Language!" Grams calls out, but she gives me a wink and a thumbs up.

Justin shakes his head and moves over for Uncle Don to come in, but he won't drop it. "I would have helped you in the end though."

"You believe this guy, Uncle Don?"

Don laughs and gives me a bear hug, then calls after Justin, "He knows you!"

"Yeah yeah," he grumbles, heading for Jason to give *him* shit, instead.

Marie, Anna, Jocelyn and Mom won't stop asking Rachel everything about her. I see this and come up behind her, telling them, "Okay, ladies. There's lots of time for that. Right Jake?"

Jake laughs, holding Drew's hand. "Let's eat!"

The crowd breaks off in approval, heading for the food table while talking, their conversations overlapping. Everyone's happy and it's gonna be a hell of a party.

Dad parts the crowd to come to us. Rachel and I

stiffen slightly but we both knew today we'd be facing him.

"Congratulations."

Rachel quietly says, "Thank you, Mr. Cocker."

He holds her eyes, his full of regret. Glancing around to make sure we're out of earshot, Dad quietly tells her, "I'm very sorry."

She nods. "It was a long time ago."

He takes this in knowing she's being polite. But he's hoping there might be a light at the end of this where she's able to put it behind her that she might have been his, and he never claimed her.

He steps away, nodding to me. I glance behind him to see Mom telling Jason to hand back the fresh ginger ale. He's objecting as she's pulling the pitcher from his hands.

"No, you can't have this whole thing. You have to share! Take this straw back."

Chuckling I turn to Rachel who's watching the scene before her. "I can't believe this is going to be my family now."

I pull her to me and privately tell her, "I love you."

"I love you, too," she whispers, gazing into my eyes like everyone vanished, the flower pressed against my back as she holds me. "You remembered the poem."

"Well, it's not exactly a poem."

"Oh, you know what I mean!"

Chuckling under my breath, I kiss her. "I did. Because I meant it. Pretty easy to remember the truth."

This makes Rachel's eyes darken. Her voice is almost inaudible as she asks, "The truth... Jaxson, how will my parents be able to be at one of these?"

Licking my lips in thought, I admit, "I don't know. Maybe we'll have a talk with them. I want to believe they can be trusted around each other, Ellen and my dad, but until I do..."

"I know," she whispers, burrowing into my chest. "Let's hope what they say is true, that time heals all wounds."

Watching my mother smiling as she carries her plate to the table, I wonder if it can.

I've given a lot of thought to what my dad said. If this affair had happened yesterday, or even five years ago I would have no doubts over what to do. But as I watch my family talking, laughing, and dishing out food, I picture what this scene would look like if I exposed the secret. Marie and Don wouldn't be here, they'd be with Dad. Jake would have to go there because Don is his boss, but he'd hate it *and* Dad. And then he'd come over here, his time split.

The twins would shun him.

None of my brothers would forgive Dad.

And Mom would be devastated.

All of this togetherness would disappear.

For now I'll keep my knowledge of his secret quiet. But if it ever comes out, I'll have to confess to Mom that I knew. And why I didn't tell her.

"You hungry, Rach?"

Pressed into me, she nods and inhales, stepping back to smile at the sunflower. "Very."

"Let's eat." But she touches my arm to hold me back. "What is it?"

"Thank you for punching Ryan. Twice."

Smirking, I lead her to the table. "You want me to do it again?"

On a growing smile, she shakes her head, our fingers entwining. "Nah…I think two times a charm."

"That's not how the saying goes."

"You couldn't let that slip by," she chuckles.

"Never." I kiss her fingertips, smiling in the knowledge that I'm ready to give her a hard time for the rest of her life.

38

RACHEL

Two years later.

"Sylvia, what time are they getting here?" I ask while folding fresh lavender-scented blankets.

My best friend glances up from her hand-written schedule and pushes curly hair back from her brown eyes. "Noon is the orientation. Why?"

"Just wondering," I breathe, feeling odd. "I might need to take a Tums or something."

She tilts her head then rises up from the patio chair, the sign Sunflower Ranch Retreat Center framing the top of her head. It's a gorgeous day so we decided to work outside this morning.

"Rachel..." she whispers, like she's trying to

273

understand something. "Are you feeling nauseous?"

I blink at her and lower my stare to the limestone porch Jaxson designed. It's cool to the touch no matter how hot the sun gets, so we can sit out here, walk barefoot, and there are no problems.

"Oh my God. I am."

"Wait here!" She runs inside and I follow her as she head for the stairs to her room. When she decided to leave the dog-eat-dog retail world to come run this retreat with me, Jaxson designed a bedroom larger than the guest ones for her to call home. "I have a pregnancy test!"

"Why do you have a pregnancy test?"

Before she alights the stairs, she throws me a look. "I get action, girl. You know I do."

Laughing and nervous, I wait for her to return. I'm tapping my foot as I call up, "Hurry!!"

Rushing to the kitchen where I left my phone by the toaster when I made my bagel and cream cheese, I start to dial Jaxson, then stop.

What if I'm not? I don't want to get him excited and then follow that up with disappointment. Staring at it I realize if I am pregnant, he will want to be here.

When he answers the phone after a couple rings, I whisper, "Jaxson?"

"Hey beautiful. Getting the tanks ready for the guys."

"Can it wait?"

He pauses. "Sure. Something wrong? Is the toilet leaking again?"

Smiling I stare out the window to our home in the far distance. "Where are you right now?"

"In the barn."

"Oh, I'm looking at the house and trying to picture you in it."

He chuckles then asks in a deeper voice, "What's going on, baby?"

Glancing to where Sylvia is running down the stairs swinging an unopened box in her hand, I smile. "I'm about to take a pregnancy test and wanted to know if you would like to come out and play."

At first there's silence on the line. "I'll be right there."

"I was just about to tell you to call him," she smiles as I set the phone down.

Exhaling, I rest my backside against the counter, bending my jeans at the knee. "Jett just told Jaxson they're pregnant. I know Jaxson was jealous. But Syl...wouldn't it be too much of a coincidence if I am, too?"

She rolls her eyes. "With the amount of sex you two have I'm surprised you don't have five babies already!"

That cracks me up. "Give me that thing."

She hands it to me but doesn't let go. We're standing

here staring at each other, both with our hands on potential joy. "Rach, you realize this time is very different from the last."

God I love friends.

"Yes. Very different."

She lets go, satisfied that life has turned out for the better. After all that drama it's a relief to know the turns I made led me to here.

The door bursts open and Jaxson runs in the room, throwing his cowboy hat on the ground. "Did you take it?"

Smiling, I answer, "Not yet."

He waves me toward the bathroom. "Come on!"

"God, I love it when you say that," I murmur, walking to take his hand. "Sylvia, come with. You guys are going to wait outside. No, Jaxson, don't make that face. I'm not peeing on this thing with you in the room."

"Grrrr."

"Did you just say, grrrr?"

"I did."

"Okay, but you're still not coming in. Want to open this for me?"

He takes the package and rips it to shreds, handing me the stick. "Holy shit."

I give him a kiss while Sylvia clasps her hands and bounces, "I'm so nervous!"

I disappear in there and come out a moment later.

"Well?" my husband demands.

"It takes a couple minutes for the results." I hold it up. "Sorry, it's a little damp."

Sylvia loses it laughing and Jaxson just frowns in concentration like staring at the plastic test strip will make it work faster.

We watch as the positive symbol slowly appears. My lips part and Jaxson steps forward.

"That's a plus sign. There's no way those fuckers would make a plus sign mean not pregnant."

"No, they wouldn't," I whisper looking at him with meaning.

"We're going to have a baby?"

"Maybe," I breathe, remembering the miscarriage and locking eyes with Sylvia who was with me through that hell.

Jaxson pulls me to him. "Stop. I know what you're thinking."

"My mother had three miscarriages."

"Your mother wasn't doing yoga and meditation and drinking ginger root every day either. You're in the best health you've ever been in."

I search his hopeful eyes. "Jaxson, even healthy women lose children."

He grabs my chin. "If you lose this one, we'll try again.

277

And again. And again. I have strong seed…and we will be parents someday, okay?"

I have to smile at his ego, and his kindness. "Okay."

"Hello?!" a familiar female voice calls in.

Cora Williamson strolls in wearing flip-flops and yoga pants under a baggy t-shirt with a smoothie in her hand. "Sorry I'm late. Fucking traffic in Atlanta is getting worse than Los Angeles!"

"Look!" I cry out, holding up the stick.

She takes one look at it, throws up her hands and sends pink smoothie juice all over the room. Running forward she cries out, "Oh my God! You're pregnant!!" We hug and then she turns to Jaxson, hitting his stomach. "Look at you! Jaxson Cocker's gonna be a daddy!! Won't the cows be jealous?"

He just crosses his arms and grins at her. "Fuck you, Cora."

She laughs and goes to hug Sylvia hello. "Isn't it great?"

"So great. You bring the gift certificates?"

"Yep, they're in the car. Come with me." They head out and leave my husband and I alone.

When she came to finalize the partnership sale, Cora and I started up right where we left off in elementary school, our friendship easy and fun.

Mr. Jarvis's wife Liana passed away just after we opened, but she was able to see it. We knew she was sick, and it was a gift for all of us to be able to show her the place whose conception had originated with her wanting to help people.

Liana asked that we have one month a year where underprivileged children could come and learn meditation to help them make better decisions for their futures even under the duress of poverty. She explained that many schools in low-income communities have begun implementing this, so we began a month-long summer camp in her name: Liana's Children.

The first one took place after she passed, but Sylvia, Cora, Jaxson, and I all lit a candle for the first night.

I wasn't surprised when Sylvia hit it off immediately with Cora. They're both a little wild but in that balanced sort of way, where there's a night every week or so, during which they hit the wine bottle too hard, sharing stories and laughing their asses off. Happy to say I join them.

Seeing what we were doing inspired Cora to come work with us part time. She still does commercial real estate because she loves the money and the 'win' but enrolling to become a certified yoga teacher has changed her life in many ways. Like she hardly ever wears heels now, says they're bad for Chi, the eternal life force that runs through us all.

I haven't taken it that far. But she was always a little excessive.

Jaxson walks the stick over to the sink. "If I wash this off, can we frame it?"

"God no!" I laugh. "Don't even!"

He chuckles and throws it in the trash, walking back to slip his arms around my lower back. As if on cue I lace mine around his thick neck. Over the past couple years we've often talked this way, discussing ideas. Most of our planning for how to build the retreat was done with us standing like this.

He smiles down at me. "Please don't name this baby with a 'J.'"

Laughing, I shake my head a little. "Your mom just got the granddaughter she wanted in Emma. Maybe we'll give her a grandson. How about Herbert?"

"Herbert?!! Absolutely. Or Melvis."

"Burger?"

"No, we'll name our son Ron. Since Harry got Hermione here." He's grinning. "Throw the kid a bone."

"No. We won't. But how about William?"

Jaxson cocks his head. "Why William?"

Rising up on my toes to kiss him, I whisper against his lips, "Shakespeare."

"Oh shit, I love it," he smiles, kissing me once. "But it's too fucking cute, so no. I say we go with…Ben."

Something happens in my core when he says that name. Like it's right, and it's already happened. With a strange sensation in my heart I feel tears rise up. "Ben. I love that name. Let's call our boy Ben."

Jaxson kisses me deeply and doesn't stop until my girlfriends come back inside and hoot at us. Laughing apart Jaxson mutters, "Too much estrogen on this property. Hope Ben gets here quick." He gives me a peck. "I have to get the milk tank ready. They're on their way."

"Okay, handsome."

As he walks over to pick up his hat, he points to the spilled smoothie. Cora throws up her hands like, *I know! I'll get it.* Before Jaxson leaves, he slips the cowboy hat on his head and glances back to me, holding my eyes a beat as he tugs it in place with his fingers on the rim. "I love you, Rachel."

"I love you, too," I smile.

Before all the healing I've done, the retreats, personal growth, coming here and getting in touch with nature, I might not have trusted my women's intuition as much as I do today. But as I watch my husband leave, there is a feeling inside me I can't deny. This baby will make it. And his name will be Ben.

THE END.

COCKER BROTHERS SERIES NOTE

I decided to write bonus chapters for this entire series, scenes that take place years after each book ends so you can experience what happens to these wonderful characters later. For Cocky Roomie, we get to meet their three children. Cocky Cowboy, we get to meet Ben. They're very fun, include more sexy scenes, and can only be accessed by eBook downloads at this time, when you sign up for private club's newsletter. The Kindle app is free for any device, and I also offer Epubs and PDFs.

You can access these through the signup button on my FB Page:

http://facebook.com/authorfaleenahopkins

Enjoy!
Xx, Faleena Hopkins

TO GET IN TOUCH:

www. AuthorFaleenaHopkins.com

http://facebook.com/authorfaleenahopkins
(mailing list link is there under: Signup)

Twitter and Instagram: @faleenahopkins

Pinterest: FaleenaMHopkins
(there is a board dedicated to this series)

To learn more about my acting/filmmaking career:
http://imdb.me/faleenahopkins

BY FALEENA HOPKINS

Cocky Roomie
Cocky Biker
Cocky Cowboy
Cocky Romantic
(Senator and Soldier, en route)

You Don't Know Me

Anything For You Series:
Changing For You
Reaching For You
Searching For You

Werewolves Of Chicago: Curragh
Werewolves Of Chicago: Howard
Werewolves Of Chicago: Xavier

Werewolves Of New York: Nathaniel
Werewolves Of New York: Eli
Werewolves Of New York: Darik
Werewolves Of New York: Dontae

Fire Nectar Vampires: The Choice
Fire Nectar Vampires: The Elders

Faleena Hopkins

ABOUT THE AUTHOR

Faleena Hopkins published her first novel in May of 2013 and due to the warm reception of her stories, was able to quit her day-job as a professional portrait photographer by September of that year to write full time.

A California native and a Los Angeles resident for twenty-three years, she moved to Atlanta, GA in December 2015 to write love stories and prepare filming for her first independent feature film. This is where the Cocker Brothers series was inspired.

Also an actress for over twenty years, her work has been praised in reviews by the Los Angeles Times, Variety and Hollywood Reporter and she intends to direct and star in her first movie, to keep pushing the boundaries of what people say she can and cannot do.

The bracelet she wears every day bears the engraving: *She believed she could so she did.* Inspiring others to follow their dreams is a big part of her passion and she regularly helps authors self-publish their way to success by sharing how she was able to get where she is, and the mistakes she navigated along the way.

Made in the USA
Middletown, DE
13 January 2018